# OF FORGIVING
# HEARTS

S.A. Pring

 FriesenPress

Suite 300 - 990 Fort St
Victoria, BC, V8V 3K2
Canada

www.friesenpress.com

ISBN
978-1-5255-1642-9 (Hardcover)
978-1-5255-1643-6 (Paperback)
978-1-5255-1644-3 (eBook)

*1. FICTION*

Distributed to the trade by The Ingram Book Company

"Mickey," came the deep, whispery voice through the darkness.

In her cot by a large cathedral window, five-year-old Mickey Jenson stirred from sleep.

"Mickey," came the whisper again.

"Who is it?" Mickey asked, now fully awake.

"Come to me, Mickey."

Mickey was not afraid. There was a familiar quality to the voice, though she couldn't quite place it. Drawing back the covers, she got out of bed and moved silently past the other cots toward the door through the thick darkness. Her white cotton nightie swayed freely about her ankles.

"Mickey." There was a pleading quality to the whisper now.

Mickey left the room and started down the back steps to the kitchen. All was dark; the only light was that of the moon shining benignly in through the window over the sink. No one was in the kitchen, and Mickey was puzzled. Wide eyed in the darkness, her five-year-old curiosity peaking, she discovered that the cellar door was open. She didn't want to go down there. The other girls said there was a monster there that only came out at night. They said it ate bad little girls who didn't go to bed when they were supposed to.

"Mickey?" came the whisper again. "Aren't you going to come and play with me?"

"I'm ascared of monsters," she whimpered softly.

"It's okay, there are no monsters down here."

"Are you sure?"

"Yes."

Mickey moved to the top of the cellar stairs, and as she did the faint, sweet odour of pipe smoke filled the air. "Danny? Danny, is that you?" she said.

"Yes, Mickey, its Danny."

Her fears lost, Mickey started down the stairs.

"But, Danny, why are you whispering?"

"Because it's part of the game."

"O-kee-doe-kee, Danny, I like whisper games." Mickey whispered back. It was more of a croak, like only a five-year-old child could summon, as she descended deeper into the darkness at the foot of the stairs until her bare feet touched the uneven concrete of the cellar floor.

"Danny, where are you? I can't see nothing," she asked, blindly pawing the air.

"I'm right here, Mickey. Here, take me hand." Out of the blackness, his huge paw-like hand closed around the fragile frame of hers.

"Danny, can we turn a light on? It's awfully dark down here."

"No, Mickey." He paused. "That's not part of the game." He led her toward the entrance of the sub- basement.

Mickey Jenson never saw the light of day again.

***

Like a poison in the blood creeping toward the heart of a weakened host, the wall above an overtaxed wall socket on the third floor darkened, tracing the path of the ancient wiring. It was a silent malignancy gone unnoticed for far too long to prevent the death of the patient.

The white-papered walls began to smoke. There was a pop, a spark, and all at once the wall gave way to flame. Decades' old wood, paint and floor varnish fueled the beast as it seemed now to stalk the sleeping inhabitants of the ancient dwelling…

"Hurry along, now, children, quickly now!" urged the stout, mean-looking Miss Windsor, who was standing at the top of the back stairs.

"The stairs to the third floor are gone! I can't get to the other children!" screamed someone else. The face belonging to the voice was hidden in the confusion of billowing grey smoke.

"I'll see to them!" Miss Windsor shouted, her voice muted by the roar of the flames. "You get these three out."

Smoke like dirty cotton funnelled waist high through the corridor, bleeding into the stairwell of the third floor, where the fire had already pushed out the windows, creating its own ventilation. Ugly fiery tongues licked the outside brick, charring it black and edging closer to the eves and the roof beyond.

Barring the stairs was a wall of flame. Through the flames, the choking screams of children penetrated the smoke, but their cries were in vain. They were completely isolated by flame and now their fate rested in the hands of God. He alone could save them now.

Flames roared across the ceiling. The white paper on the walls darkened to brown and then exploded in an angry array of orange, yellow and blood-red. The smoke turned from grey to a thick oppressive black.

Partway down the back steps, the youngest of the three children, Delse, broke free of the woman's vice-like grip and scrambled for the top of the stairs. "Mickey! Mickey, where are you?" she called as she went. She had just reached the top of the stairs when Miss Windsor appeared in the smoke-filled hallway and seized her into powerful arms.

"No!" Delse screamed. "Mickey, I have to find Mickey!"

"She isn't here, child!" Miss Windsor shouted to make herself heard over the roaring blaze.

"She is so!" Delse bawled. "I saw her!" Delse was inconsolable. Miss Windsor ignored the child's cries and pushed ahead down the stairs and outside to safety where the others were already waiting.

The windows on the second floor erupted outward in synchronous glass-laden explosions.

Two middle-aged woman clutching each other tightly stumbled outside and down the steps from the kitchen and walked toward the fire engines. Inside, the remaining windows were alight in the dizzy dance of the inferno raging within.

The screams of trapped children filled the night. The sound of something heavy falling silenced the screams, leaving only the roar of the fire and the crackling of decades' old wood.

The stars in the night sky were now well hidden behind a mask of smoke. The fire seemed quenchless. The efforts of the many firemen rushing this way and that were completely in vain. To all who watched, it must have appeared that hell itself had opened up, intent upon swallowing this isolated haven for unwanted children. The blaze raged on.

On the lawn, beyond the blockade of fire department vehicles, stood three small girls. Their pale faces were smudged with soot. Their eyes were wide and unseeing, filled with the terror only fire combined with death can provide.

# PART 1
## Collingwood, Ontario

-Twenty years later-

"Man is the only creature that spends its entire life trying to become what it already is."

Unknown

# CHAPTER 1

Smudges of rusty brown, red and gold, all but gone now from the branches of trees towering nearby, lay scattered through the ditches and fields, partially obscuring the surface of the road. Icy water from recent heavy rains flooded the ditches, washing autumn's earth-toned foliage to the catch basins far below at the foot of Blue Mountain. The sky, grey and foreboding, streaked with hues of copper, promised more of the same before too much longer. Nearby farmers' fields, once brimming with lush greens and silk tassels, now lay bare. Their rich, dark and muddy soil displayed only the stubble of last season's corn, soon to be ploughed under that it might return to the ground whence it came.

Of all the seasons, this was Meagan's favourite. Everything seemed so much truer to her. She saw none of the omens of death most associated with this time of the year. Meagan Bathurst was an artist. She hadn't sold anything yet, but still found great solace in coming out here to the countryside and painting.

As she walked by the side of the road toward an ancient squatter's dwelling, a large, rather cumbersome looking blue Oldsmobile lumbered past, sending a fury of wind devils to ravage the leaves by the side of the road.

Meagan wasn't what one might call a drop-dead beauty. There was more of a handsome quality about her. Her hair was a constant barrage of untameable red, worn long and pulled back carelessly into a loose ponytail that threatened to come loose at any moment. Her face was round, and her complexion darker than one might attribute to a redhead. Her eyes, pale orbs of green-blue, set her apart; they were slightly sad, yet capable of exploding with insatiable wonderment of the world around her.

The old house now before her, she positioned herself behind the collapsible easel and studied her subject. There wasn't much to see— just a tiny, one-room shack with a loft. The ground floor had long since rotted away, and there were weather-stained wood siding and blackened openings where single panes once fought off the cold of Georgian winters. And there were shutters, but mind you, their only remaining legacy were the hand-made, metal brackets once holding them in place. Behind and to the left of the house, separating it from the road, an explosion of evergreen and a lone lightning-stunted birch reared up from the rocky soil along the ditch.

With each sweep of the knife the scene before her came to life. As it did, Meagan became more and more a part of it until the two were one and the same. She imagined what it must have been like growing up in those times. The work was harder, the fun more innocent, and there was a sense of hope and accomplishment untarnished by tax-grubbing governments. She envied those early settlers and wished life today could somehow be as simple. Back then, parents treasured their children. Back then, people could be trusted. And back then, people didn't give their babies away to total strangers.

Meagan had been adopted at age five by the Bathursts, though lived completely unaware they weren't her true parents until she was twenty. Now she was twenty-five, living on her own, and determined to discover who her birth parents were.

In the beginning, Tina and Craig—it didn't feel right calling them Mom and Dad

anymore— weren't pleased with the idea. Perhaps that was why they put off telling her for so long, for fear of losing her, alienating her from them. Whatever their intent, the result was the same. She did feel alienated and alone. Knowing now that a part of her life was missing, she needed to discover it for herself. Tina and Craig would be no help. They didn't approve of her actions, and if they did know who her parents were, they weren't telling.

The afternoon was wearing on. The sky was taking on an even more aggressive posture when finally she decided enough had been done for one day. Packing up her gear, she started back toward her car, which was parked some two hundred yards away at the base of the steep mountain road, leaving the lonely structure to its simplistic past.

As she drove back toward the town of Collingwood, the streets looked naked, void of warmth. She once felt so safe and content here, but no longer. For now, although she had lived in Collingwood longer than she could remember, she suddenly felt she no longer belonged. Somewhere on the other side of those wondrous mountains to the south were her roots, her real home and family. Everything around her now dulled in the shadow of her expectations.

Passing the street where Tina and Craig lived, she was tempted to stop in on them, see how they were doing, but decided against it. The visits always ended the same way. While there were times when Tina swayed toward Meagan's way of thinking, Craig was always the holdout. Meagan felt justified in her quest, as did Craig in his opposition to it. Clearly, there was nothing like the forbidden knowledge of hidden truths when it came to dissecting a family.

The truth be known, Meagan had not intended her quest to cause the rift that had formed. She only wanted to know who she was. And when she asked about her past they would respond in the well-rehearsed, stone-wall fashion she had grown so accustomed to through the years: "*You're Meagan Bathurst and you're our daughter and that should be good enough for you!*"

However, for Meagan, it was not.

How could they even think it might be?

The first drops of yet another storm began falling as Meagan left her car and started toward her building.

She lived in a third-floor loft above a Chinese food restaurant that had been made over into an apartment. The restaurant had been shut down by the health inspector a year ago and had never reopened. Her loft was quiet, for the most part, and offered a great deal of space where she could work on her paintings. Best of all, the rent was cheap.

She turned the key in the lock and slid the door open as the strong, sharp odour of burnt coffee filled her senses. *Damn*, she realized...she forgot to turn the darn coffee maker off again. It had been on all day, and now all that remained was a scabby black tar crusted to the bottom of the pot. She turned it off and was about to leave the kitchen when the flashing red light on her telephone answering machine caught her attention. She pushed the appropriate button and headed for the bedroom while the messages played.

BEEP. "This is your mother... I mean. Tina. calling. We'll be eating at four and you're welcome to join us. Call me later, okay? I love you, sweetie."

So much for that invite; it was already pushing six.

BEEP. "Meagan, are you there?" This call was from Bruce Stewart, the private investigator she hired to aid in her search for her real parents. "I think I've found something. Call me when you get in." By this time, Meagan was standing over the machine.

BEEP. "For Christ's sake, Meagan, its 4: 30, where are you? This is important!" It was Bruce again.

His messages sent Meagan into a tail spin. It was after business hours, and, as she suspected, there was no answer at his office. She would have to wait until morning to find out what he had to tell her.

Sleep would not come easily.

# CHAPTER 2

As she knew it would, sleep eluded her and now she found herself walking along Collingwood's main street, which was referred to by locals as the Promenade. All was quiet, and the first appearance of flurries could be seen drifting down in the glow of the street lamps.

The three area bars had released their patrons almost two hours earlier and now all but the most intoxicated had found their beds for the night. The rest would soon be picked up and taken to the local drunk tank. There they could sleep off their reason for living.

A large snowflake settled upon her left eyelash. She didn't protest its presence. *Where was she really from?* she wondered silently, once again. This was one of the questions that had deprived her of rest for the past five years. Finally, it appeared she would find the answer. However, with its answer so close, another question filled her with concern: what would she find there? Would there be open arms and tearful greetings, or simply more questions to which the answer were also hidden? The morning would provide the start.

Two blocks behind her skulked a large black limousine, its headlights off. The tactic was fruitless even at three in the morning. The Promenade was the best-lit street in town. A rear door opened and out stepped a tall blonde man wearing a heavy wool trench coat. He mirrored the car's movement behind Meagan.

Glancing over her shoulder, Meagan noticed the car and it stifled headlights. *Curious*, she thought. The man walking beside it came into view. Her eyes narrowed. Normally the sight of such a fancy car on Collingwood's main street would have brought envious gazes from all who saw it, including Meagan, but something wasn't right about this one. Perhaps it was the hour, or maybe just her mood, but something seemed off.

Testing her theory, Meagan ducked into an alley that opened onto Pine Street. Emerging from the alley, she chanced a backward glance. The silhouette of a large man filled the alley behind her. She could see the limousine creeping around the corner. Her pulse quickened. Adrenaline throbbed unchecked through her body. Her pace increased. There was an all- night coffee shop nearby. She would go there. She'd be safe there.

The coffee shop was almost empty. Meagan ordered and quickly took a seat at the back. Through the glass she could see the limousine pull up in front and stop. Her frame stiffened as the man in the wool overcoat got out and started toward the door. Was he following her? *Just stay cool, see what he's up to*, she reassured herself silently. *He won't try anything in here.*

The bell over the door heralded his arrival. Meagan's pulse raced faster with expectant fear. Then, to her surprise, he simply ordered two take-out coffees and left the shop.

She scolded herself out loud: "What's got you so damned jumpy all of a sudden?"as though speaking to someone on the other side of the table. Feeling shaken and a little foolish, she pushed the untouched cup of coffee away and left the shop.

The snow, falling much heavier now, promised to dump at least six centimetres on the town before morning. Soon the ski resorts would begin their snow-making operations, then, as happened every winter, the town's population would swell to four times its normal size with skiing enthusiasts from across the province. Once they arrived, the peaceful town of Collingwood would cease to exist until March when the snows gave way once more in an explosion of green.

The limousine was back.

There was no doubt in her mind; not this time.

Who were they?

"Stay cool, you're almost home," she coached softly.

The limousine drew in closer. The car's engine roared in her ears.

Fear raged out of control. When she reached her house, Meagan sprinted to the main door, and once through it she sent the dead bolt tumbling home. After soaring up two flights of stairs to her apartment, she bolted herself in.

One small lamp glowed beside the window overlooking the street. Even in its stifled glow, she felt exposed. It would cast shadows. If they were watching the windows from the street, they would be able to trace her movements. She crossed to the light and quickly shut it off. Her body trembled as she peered expectantly down into the street. The limousine idled just below her window. She couldn't see the man in the wool coat, but she knew he was there. She stared down at the car, refusing to let it out of her sight. It began to move and soon rounded the corner out of sight.

Rolling away from the window, a sigh of relief escaped her lips. She crept quietly into the kitchen, as though someone might be listening, and poured herself a double rye. She gulped it down greedily, trying to force a reluctant calm. After two more of the same, her hands stopped shaking. Perhaps now sleep would not be so elusive.

**"Okay, try it again," Meagan said to a young redheaded girl seated behind the wheel.**

**Who was she? ...Someone familiar, yes, but who? ... Nothing ... the engine refused to start...Suddenly, flames... The engine was on fire! ... The little girl, I have to get her out...Too late! The car exploded, throwing Meagan backwards through the wall of the barn... Through, as though she were only air ... Passing right through the wall. How did I get over here? She should be in the barn, but instead she stood twenty-five yards from the car on the driver's side. Moving now... not walking... floating... Moving closer to the car... No sound... White sheets of flame... No heat...**

**Windshield shattered.... no smell...Fire everywhere; one little girl inside.**

**Wait! There are two adults, yes, clearly, adult-size. Who are they?**

**Faces coming clearer now... What! ...No, it can't be!**

Meagan's eyes darted open with fright. She hated having nightmares, and this was the third time this week.

# CHAPTER 3

With the warmth of the noon sun the snow from the night before faded, leaving the uncut grass of Bayside Park to stir in the icy northwesterly. During the warmer months, the park was alive with the shrill voices of children and barking dogs. Now the only voice was that of the wind rushing in off the bay.

Meagan and Bruce Stewart were alone in the park that day, their collars turned up against the chill.

Stewart would have preferred to conduct this meeting in the warmth of his office, but Meagan had insisted.

The conversation wasn't at all what Stewart thought it would be. He had come up with the name of the orphanage—the Forgiving Hearts—where Meagan stayed prior to being adopted. It wasn't much, but it was a place to start. However, now someone was following Meagan, and his discovery would have to wait.

"You don't have any idea why these guys were following you? Did you … would you recognize them again if you saw them? "Stewart asked, trying to make sense of Meagan's tale.

"Sure, I could, but what would that accomplish? Next time, if there even is a next time, I might not be so lucky. Hell, I don't really know they intended to harm me! For all I know, they were just a couple of drunks who happen to like redheads, saw me, and decided it was playtime," she sighed, pushing her right hand through her wind-tangled hair and holding it to the base of her neck. She gazed out over the white capped waters of the bay.

"'Don't dismiss it so quickly," he warned. "Drunks don't drive around in limousines.... Not in this town, anyway."

"Oh, yeah.... What the hell should I do, huh? Hire a bodyguard? That's idiotic and you know it! I'm more than capable of taking care of myself."

"Really? That explains why you sounded so frantic when you called me this morning," Stewart quipped.

"I told you, I had a bad dream," she said.

'Bull!" he snapped. "Meagan, I haven't known you all that long, but I think I have a pretty good idea of what you're all about. And I don't believe you were upset by a bad dream. Now, unless you want to fire … do you?"

"No."

"Fine! From here on out we do things my way. Is that clear?" he said.

"Okay, Tarzan. What's your first move?"

"Our first move is to pay a visit to the cops and take a peek at their mug shots. Maybe we can get a line on the guy you saw last night."

"I didn't think cops liked private investigators."

"Mostly they don't, but my sister married one. Man, can she be a bitch when someone is mean to her baby brother." He chuckled softly, turning toward the car.

They would come back for her car later.

Concealed by the bushes at the end of the clearing stood the blonde man in the wool overcoat. His name was Pete Robertson. He was a tall, attractive man willing to do just about anything for the right price. Loving a challenge, he had taken on this assignment with the zeal of a boy scout.

He received his instructions four days earlier following a brief phone conversation with his unseen employer. Though he had never met the lady, his contacts assured him she was on the level and to take the hire.

Shortly thereafter, a briefcase-sized parcel arrived by courier. In it were three photographs of three different young women with the necessary information written on the back of each one. Also in the case was a list of explicit instructions and $250,000.00, the balance to be paid upon completion of the assignment. The driver was a perk, supplied by his employer, and knew nothing of the operation. Pete felt it best if it remained that way.

He remained completely still until they left the lot. Only once they were gone did he leave the cover of the bushes and move toward Meagan's car. Once there, he removed a small homing device from his pocket and attached it to the rear wheel well. The limousine returned and he was gone, no one the wiser— he had ever been there.

"Why are you wiring the chick's car? I hate like shit always being kept in the dark," the young man seated behind the wheel complained.

"Just drive the car."

"'For Christ's sakes!" the driver muttered. "Where to now?"

"Back to the hotel. I want to be packed and on the highway within the hour."

"Huh? Where we going?"

"Sarnia."

"What's in Sarnia?"

"Contestants number two and three." Pete smirked.

# CHAPTER 4

Stewart and Meagan entered the police station through the rear parking garage, which was usually left open throughout the day. This was where the police brought in those who had been arrested, and it was the only entrance Stewart had ever been through. It wouldn't have felt right walking through the front doors … at least, not intentionally. Once inside, he directed her to a row of eight cubicles and instructed her to have a seat. No one seemed to be around. As usual, only a minimal staff manned the headquarters while eight others fielded calls from the street.

"I'll be right back," he said, moving into the next room in search of his brother-in-law. It wasn't long before he spotted Denis Tanning and made his way toward him. At that same instant, Tanning noticed Stewart approaching. He prepared himself for the touch he knew was coming.

"Hey, Deny, how's it hanging?" he asked, a little too heartfelt, Stewart thought afterward.

"I'm fine Bruce. What can I do for you this time?" A definite tone of suspicion clouded his words.

"Well, Deny, as a matter of fact, I need a client of mine to take a look through the picture books you keep in the filling cabinet in the dispatcher's office. "

"Sorry, buddy, you know I can't do that. It's against the rules."

"Are you sure?"

"Yeah, Bruce, I'm sure"

"Hey, well, if you can't, you can't. That's all there is to that, right?"

It occurred to Tanning that his loving brother-in-law was giving up far too easily. He knew it wasn't over yet. Turning to leave, Stewart walked a couple of steps before half turning and looking back at Tanning.

"Oh, by the way, what type of wine should I bring tonight? Yeah, didn't sis tell you? She invited me over for dinner tonight."

There it was … the hook. Tanning knew it had to be there somewhere and he was right. Stewart was one conniving son-of-a-bitch, Tanning thought, smiling. One choice word from little brother and instantly life would take on a whole new definition of hell.

"Well, I'll figure it out. See you tonight." Stewart smiled, turning to leave.

Tanning was almost back to where he had left Meagan when, thinking more of the possibility of not having a sex life for the foreseeable future than of departmental rule, came striding up behind with the mug books in hand. "Better make it a quick peak. Then get the hell out of here. Do you hear me?"

"Thanks, Deny," Stewart said. He loved it when he got his way. "See you tonight."

"Yeah, yeah." Tanning stormed off in disgust, wishing his dick didn't play such an important role in life. Stopping mid-thought, he took the wish back.

Twenty minutes and two books later Meagan was unable to pick out a single face from the pages.

"See, I told you. Maybe the guy wasn't really following me after all," she said, giving up.

"Or maybe he just hasn't been picked up for anything yet," Stewart rebuked.

She was tired and in no mood for any more cops and robbers. "Well, tell you what. You stay here and browbeat your brother-in-law; you seem to enjoy doing that sort of thing. Me, I'm going home. I'm tired and I have one bitch of a headache."

"Alright, let's go!"

"You don't have to come if you don't want to."

"Have you forgotten? We left your car at the park?"

"Shit! I completely forgot about that," Meagan muttered.

Stewart, deciding to display one of his so-called few redeeming qualities, said nothing. He simply opened the door and held it for her as they started toward the car.

# CHAPTER 5

Sarnia, Ontario

Delse Collier leaned across the table. She knew the three guys standing against the wall watching were getting a full view of her ass plastered into the skin-tight blue jeans. She wore them for this very reason.

"Eight ball, side pocket." The shot was in plain sight for all to see, yet none did. They were content to watch the gentle curves of Delse's butt as she leaned precariously over the table for a better shot.

The ball fell as instructed.

"I believe that means you lose." She smirked, scooping a stack of ten five-dollar bills from the rim of the table and inserting them between her full breasts, which were held loosely in place by a less than modest black tank.

"Delse, darling, if 1 didn't know better, I'd swear I was just hustled," local barfly Russel Krill accused.

"Well, maybe someday you will," she said, toying with him. She took the last pull on her beer.

"How about a rematch?" Krill pressed. There was an edge to his tone.

She dismissed it. "Sorry guy, but I don't give lessons," she said. "Besides, I gotta head." There were the usual protests from those who had lost to her, but she paid no mind.

All at once the thrill of the win faded. As she turned toward the door, Krill moved to block her departure.

"I said … how about a rematch, Sweets." The edge was sharper now and not so easily ignored. The situation was growing more serious by the moment. Locals, noticing the disturbance, crowded around to see the outcome.

Krill was loving it. He made it a point to let everyone know he didn't like hustlers and what he'd do to one if he ever caught one. Often times while Delse sat at the bar listening to his drunken banter he spoke of that "look" all hustlers had, affirming he could pick one out a mile off.

Delse realized he was seeing that look in her and didn't like it much. "Listen, lard-ass,

I told you, I don't give lessons," she spat. Her jaw was firmly set, and her eyes were cold, yet full of fire.

"Hey, Krill … teach the bitch a lesson!" an unseen drunk yelled from the crowd.

"Yeah, go on. Teach her she can't get away with that shit around here!" said yet another.

With calculated ease, Delse eyed the room, looking for the weak spots. There weren't many. Krill moved closer—too close.

Her cue still lay on the table close by t. Closing her hand around it, she brought it to life with a rapid flick of the wrist. "Now, lard-ass, get out of my way before I show you a whole new use for this here stick," Delse snarled.

"Will one of you idiots take that from her?" Krill ordered.

The first of Krill's goons stepped forward from behind. It was no good. Delse could see his reflection in the bar window. A taunt thrust and he lay moaning at her feet, his hands clamped firmly between his legs.

"You're next, fatso!" she said, striding toward Krill, undaunted by his size.

Krill apparently didn't take her threat seriously. Perhaps he should have, for moments later he too found new comfort clasping his testicles as Delse made a successful bid for the door.

Cool air lifted her spirits as she soared from the bar into an unusually temperate November night and started for home. Wouldn't feel much like Christmas if they didn't get snow soon, she thought, dismissing the scuffle. Christmas—she loved the season the lights, the music. It was a time of year that could always make her glow inside, though life had often left little to glow about.

She remembered her first Christmas as Delse Collier; remembered thinking finally all the bad that was so much a part of her life to that point was over. It was the happiest time of her life. But her happiness wasn't to last.

She left home at age sixteen; if home was what you chose to call it. A drunk for a father unable to find a single kind word for her, and a mother … well Mother got out. When Delse was ten, her mother decided she didn't want to be Mommy and wife anymore, so she found the first available meal ticket and hit the road. Things went downhill from there. Delse's father had never wanted to adopt a child, but went along with the idea to save his failing marriage back in the days when he still cared about saving it.

Often Delse wondered why he allowed her to stay after his wife left. The answer was abundantly clear. Who else would cook and clean for him?

Delse hadn't been to see him in almost eight months. He was still a drunk and she really didn't feel the need to subject herself to his ever-changing moods and guilt trips. His beef was always the same. He named her as solely to blame for his wife's leaving. She knew it wasn't true. Still, it didn't make it any easier to endure.

Her hardened exterior momentarily slipping, she swiped a tear glistening in her eye before it could materialize. Folding her arms tightly across her bosom, she increased her pace.

As happened every year, the city was celebrating its Festival of Lights. The whole waterfront stood illuminated with wondrous depictions of the holiday. Lovers could be seen strolling arm in arm along gilded walkways, seemingly oblivious to its beauty, yet somehow a part of it. She envied them their closeness, their intimacy.

She stopped for a moment and watched them. She wondered if that same closeness would someday find her … and if someday she could bring herself to allow it.

When she got home she pushed the door leading into the dreary one-bedroom apartment. The room was chilly

As of this morning she lived here alone and, though it wasn't anything at all to look at, she felt safe here. The furnishings were sparse—mostly Good Will finds, and the main colour was brown.

A few strands of silver tinsel and a red bow here and there were all her unforgiving income and tips would allow. Still, it was Christmas and it wouldn't feel right if she didn't brighten the place up a bit.

She walked across the room to a small ghetto-blaster— her entertainment hub—and pressed play. Instantly the room filled with sounds of Bing Crosby's "Silver Bells." The song started halfway through, but it didn't matter; she would rewind it and play it again and again before the night was through.

Next to the tape player was a shattered eight-by-ten photograph of the man no longer in her life. He was as close to love as she had been. At least, she thought so at the time. All of that was over now. He left vowing never to return. It suited her fine. The events of that night were growing increasingly dim. As with most violent confrontations involving parting lovers, who said what first soon loses its importance—only the bruises remain. How did it start? More importantly, when did it start? Yesterday? Two weeks ago? Six months? It was difficult to nail it down exactly. Even more difficult to nail down was the reason she'd allowed it to continue for as long as she had. And what was so different about last night that it made her finally bring it to an end? Perhaps it was the hard-won lessons dealt by her adopted father. Maybe it was because she didn't want to relive the same hells as an adult that she had known as a child. Whatever the reason, it was over now.

Somewhere out there had to be a decent man; someone who would love her and need her for something more than a target for his anger. Somehow, though she couldn't say with certainty when the transformation had taken place, her Mr. Wonderful had taken on the same mystique as Santa Claus … and she had stopped believing in elves years ago.

# CHAPTER 6

Early the next morning a car horn sounded in the street. Her ride was here. She locked the door and hurried down the stairs to the street where Geoff Savage waited in his rusted Civic.

He was a good guy, she thought. Though most of the girls at the restaurant believed he was gay and steered clear, she liked him. A result of her upbringing, she learned to take her friends where she found them. Trivial matters like sexual orientation didn't concern her in the slightest. Reaching down for the door handle, she happened to glance to her left and see a large black limousine parked at the side of the road.

"Looks like someone's slumming it back there," she stated, getting in.

"Yeah, must be. That boat was there when I got here. I haven't seen anyone around it, though," Geoff returned.

They couldn't see the two figures seated behind the smoked windshield.

The limousine soon forgotten, Geoff eased the small car from the curb and started toward the restaurant.

"Makin' any plans for Christmas yet?" he asked.

"Not really. I'll probably do what I always do. Go see my old man. Help him up off the floor where he passed out the night before so he can open his present then leave and spend the rest of it alone. What about you?" she asked.

"Going over to my folks' place, I guess. Hey, how about joining us? You could come as my guest!" The request seemed genuine enough, but she couldn't except it. It wouldn't feel right.

"Yeah. right! Me with your folks. Mister and Missus White Bread of Canada …. Don't make me laugh!"

"Well, if you change your mind." At that, he pulled the Civic into the parking spot and shut it down.

It was especially busy and the morning rush went by quickly. Delse was about to start the cleanup and prepare for the lunch crowd when she noticed the sleek black limousine parked out on the street. Glancing around the room, she found almost half of the tables still occupied and wondered which of the customers had pulled up in it. What was more, why would anyone who could afford such a car bother to eat in a place like this when there were far better restaurants just down the block?

"Hey, Delse … get a move on. The food's gettin' cold!" boomed Larry Mitchell, the owner of the St. Clair Diner. He was a heavy-set man, standing not more than 5' 5", of dubious, possibly Greek ancestry, and was a tyrant to work for.

Throughout the remainder of her shift Delse went about serving her section. She kept an eye on the car and wondered who the owner could be.

Carrying a tray loaded with dirty dishes, Delse headed for the kitchen. She would ask Jean, the waitress working the other section, when she got a chance.

By the time Delse offloaded her tray and returned to the floor, three of Jean's tables were gone. The limousine was gone along with them.

The end of Delse's shift came swiftly, and she began the long walk home. She didn't mind so much. It gave her time to think. Besides, she wanted to stop and pick up a couple of items for the apartment. Cutting over to Christina Street, she passed in front of the Eaton's display window. One outfit was beautiful and held her transfixed. It was a wondrous black dress arrayed with sequins and draped with tinsel and satin ribbon. An outfit that one day, she assured herself, she would buy without worrying about the price tag.

Christina was one of the busiest streets in Sarnia, especially since the revitalization of the downtown core, though never more so than at Christmas. Throngs of shoppers mobbed the stores in search of that perfect gift and the sidewalks were crowded.

While Delse stood gazing through the glass the crowd thinned, exposing the street behind her. Soon her gaze fell not to what was behind the glass, but rather to the refection in it. There, parked at the curb, was the same black limousine she first saw outside her apartment and then again at the diner.

Pretending she hadn't noticed it, she turned and walked on. She didn't like this. Something just wasn't right about the way it kept showing up wherever she went. "You're letting yourself get carried away, Delse … time to get a grip," she murmured. After all, who would want to follow her? Why? Suddenly, visions of Krill and his gang filled her mind.

A car door slammed, catching her attention. She turned to see a tall young man wearing a grey trench step away from the car. The limousine left the curb and edged slowly through the traffic beyond the parking lane.

"Shit!" she said. "Why did he have to do that?" His actions left no room for doubt. "Okay, girl, stay cool … you can lose this sucker," she promised herself through clenched teeth.

Up ahead another crowd of people formed and stood marvelling over yet another window display. She made her way toward it. Whoever Mister Trench Coat was, he wasn't likely to try anything with so many witnesses around. At the first opportunity, she would duck into an alley and make a break for it.

At the next set of lights, not more than a block away, Geoff's rusted Civic was stopped at a red.

*Thank God!* she thought. She snapped a quick glance to see where Mister Trench Coat was and made a dash for it. The traffic light had other plans for Geoff's car, however. It had been red for quite a while before Delse noticed his car sitting there, and turned green, releasing him, before she could make it. She stopped dead. Her mouth agape, she watched as her refuge lurched away at fifty kilometres an hour.

Quickly regaining a grasp on the situation, her eyes shot back to Mister Trench Coat. He was much closer now and watching her while pretending to window shop. Their eyes met for a brief moment, Delse was sure of it. His stare was cold, showing no sign of distress at being found out. Delse stood motionless, feeling almost mesmerized by him, his presence. There was something very different about him, though she had no desire to discover what it was.

As luck would have it, she found herself standing in front of Maelley's Deli. She ducked inside. She and the owner, whose name wasn't Maelley, but Johnson, had been friends for many years. He had caught her shoplifting when she was thirteen years old and made her work for him until the merchandise was paid for. Yes, Delse Collier was an ex-con—the lure of her larceny had been a single candy bar.

"Dave, you gotta help me!" Delse announced before the bells over the door fell silent.

"Deli, how are?" bellowed the massive Scot.

"Not good. I need to use your back door," she stated. "There's a guy in a grey trench coat following me."

"Say no more, Deli. I'll keep him busy for you. Get going."

"Thanks, Dave," she said, fading into the stock room and through the back door beyond. It led into a maze of alleys and Delse knew each of them well. Minutes later she was gone, leaving Mister Trench Coat the unlucky recipient of Dave Johnson's full, undivided attention.

# CHAPTER 7

The bus was full this time around—her fourth circuit of its route through the city. With each stop the doors would open, allowing passengers on and off, and each time Delse fixed her eyes to the curb waiting to see the grey trench coat. The doors would close with no sign of him and Delse would relax into her seat once more.

She counted one hundred and thirteen passengers that afternoon. Though they varied in their mode of dress, they all bore a striking resemblance to each other. Somehow, the instant they set foot on the bus their social skills disappeared. Their faces were all different, yet mostly the same; eyes cast down, out the window or blankly straight ahead—anything to avoid looking or heaven forbid actually speaking to the person seated next to them.

There was comfort having so many people around, Delse thought. Though physical protection could not be expected, their numbers alone would be enough to deter a would-be assailant.

Twilight was settling over the city when the bus stopped and Delse stepped to the curb.

Her father's house was an older home, probably built near the end of the Second World War and showing all the signs of neglect. The lawns unkempt, uncut since late August, lay matted with soggy leaves. The wood siding was cracked and warped, its faded blue paint neglected against the elements. Even the porch, added some twenty years later, sagged. Its plywood sheeting was puffy with moisture and stained black with mildew seeping through a thin coat of white paint. The mailbox was stuffed to the point that several letters, unpaid bills mostly, had simply been tossed on the floor. At some point, they too were exposed to the elements and now were completely illegible.

Gingerly, she opened the screen door. The shattered upper pane was still not replaced from when he put his fist through it the year before. The inside door was locked. She used her key and pushed open the door. Immediately, her senses were assaulted by odours so sharp her eyes began to tear.

There was no sound. No light—the blinds were all closed. The lamps were off, and still there was that smell. "What the hell is that?" she demanded.

The dishes piled in the sink, perhaps ... no... mould could never smell like this. The fridge door was open slightly. Pulling it open fully, the stench of rotted food spilled out. "What the hell!" she murmured. Turning now, she left the kitchen and made yet another grisly discovery. Shithead, their cat, was dead, and from the looks of him, he had been for some time. His fur churned with the presence of maggots gorging themselves inside the tattered carcass. Bile rose thickly in Delse's throat. She swallowed hard, forcing it back. She didn't need to see anything more to know what had happened here. Returning to the kitchen, she picked up the phone. To her surprise, it still worked. She dialled 9-1-1.

Twenty minutes later, Delse's father was carried out, draped head to foot with an orange plastic sheet.

Standing on the sidewalk, Delse overheard two police officers talking on the porch.

"This guy's been dead for weeks!" one stated, dumbfounded, shaking his head.

"Who called it in?" the other asked.

"The daughter. She found the body."

The two of them descended the porch steps and approached her.

"We're terribly sorry for your loss, ma'am."

"Don't waste your pity. Not on him. It was bound to happen sooner or later," she intoned, her emotions masked with a heavy sheet of iron. "I gave my name, address and phone number to the cop over there. If you have anything further you need to ask me you can reach me at home. Thank you for coming so quickly."

Delse turned and walked away.

Back at her apartment, she sat resting her chin upon her knees. The drunken tyrant she knew as "Daddy" was gone. He couldn't hurt her any more.

She wondered what her real father was like. How her life might have been different had she not been adopted out. Her thoughts filled with fanciful images of a real family; a family strong in its union and loving of its members. She swept the image away.

Straightening her legs, she scootched down, placed the back of her head on the armrest and closed her eyes.

**The driveway was long, the snow deep and all but obscuring the day-old tire tracks of the car from the day before. Standing at the road, she stared at the house set a good seventy-five yards back from the highway. Its malevolence was overpowering. Three storeys of Victorian red brick with rounded turrets at every corner and lightning rods stretching skyward from each one. Twisted black rod-iron railings, seemingly protecting nothing, adorned the roof.**

**Left of the lane, close to the road, a hinged, whitewashed sign swayed haplessly in the winter wind. The lettering, in old English script, read:**

**FORGIVING HEARTS ORPHANAGE**
**BLESSED BE THOSE OF FORGIVING HEARTS.**

**Standing at the side porch now, feeling anxious. Fire! People, children screaming inside … children burning! Grasping the doorknob with both hands, Delse pulled with all of her strength, attempting to get past this barrier and inside in order to free those screaming for help beyond. Stuck … it wouldn't move; the heat welded the hinges shut. Then, movement. Just a little … inches, no more. From within, the flames licked the edges of the door. The screams … the cries from beyond the door seemed louder now. Have to get them out … have to … have to get them out! The door was open three inches now. Unseen hands from behind fell upon her shoulders …what's going on! … pulling her away. The screams … can't you hear their screams …**

Delse opened her eyes to find her living room looking the way she had left it. A bad dream, that's all, nothing more.

# CHAPTER 8

A ghost-like mist hung in the air, making the morning seem more like April than November. Mobs of children dotted the corners, awaiting the arrival of school busses coming to obstruct traffic, making the drive to work twice as long. So far, she had beaten them. There wasn't a single bus anywhere to be seen.

Her name was Julia Hart and she was a case worker with the Sarnia chapter of the Children's Aid society. Just out of school with no practical field experience, she was lucky to land the job. Funding was short, as was usually the case with social programs, making the positions harder to find. Nevertheless, she got the job and gladly made the move from her home town of London, Ontario, only a month before.

The years of study paid off. Not so, however, for many of her classmates. They were forced to give up on their dream of helping children, unable to find placements, and had to seek more sedentary lines of employment to pay the rent. Yes, she was one of the lucky ones.

It was difficult in the beginning. Living in a strange town and not knowing anyone was lonely, but it got a little easier with each passing day. She threw herself into the work like a young priest out to save the world. Her case load made her colleges shudder. They watched her with her newly acquired passion, waiting for what they referred to as *The Change*. Susan had told her about The Change—a gradual accumulation of callous forming around the senses, perverting one's purpose. Julia swore it would never happen to her. They didn't believe her.

Their negative outlook didn't bother her. She wouldn't let it, for she truly believed she could make a difference. A cliché, perhaps, but it didn't dampen her spirits. There was much more at stake in this mission she assigned herself.

She had to keep these new kids coming through the system from knowing the same hell she knew before being adopted by the Harts. The foster homes had seemed to follow one another in endless succession.

A slight breeze blew up, carrying away the mist, by the time she parked her car in the lot. Locking the door, she glanced toward the sky and breathed deeply the spring-smelling air. *Doesn't feel much like Christmas this year*, she thought, sweeping her shoulder-length blonde hair away from her face.

Inside, the offices were filled with the usual jangle of phones ringing and babies crying while parents waited with professed patience in plastic back chairs. She had barely set foot inside her partitioned-off office before Susan, a young black woman who was already looking haggard, appeared in the door-less entrance. "Mrs. Mitchell called. Tom's gone again," she announced.

"Wonderful," Julia replied. "How long this time?'

"His mother says she thinks he left sometime early this morning."

"Surprise, surprise." Julia sighed, already putting her coat back on. "Okay, if she calls back tell her I have a pretty good idea of where he might be. I'll see that he gets home safely." At that, she swept past Susan heading for the exit.

"Do you really think she will?" Susan asked cynically. Julia didn't respond. She just kept walking, throwing her arms into the air as though to say, "who knows!"

There was no doubt in her mind as she made her way through the last of the morning rush-hour traffic. She knew exactly where to find Tom.

She'd been on this case a little more than three weeks, and had already broken the first and most important rule. NEVER GET EMOTIONALLY INVOLVED was drilled into them in college, but still it made no difference. It was a stupid rule to begin with, or so she believed. Besides, this was a special case.

Tommy wasn't a bad kid. The father was not in the picture. That left only the boy's mother and a string of boyfriends, none lasting more than a few weeks. It wasn't a great situation by anyone's standards. The result was a fourteen-year-old boy who was rebellious and alone. She couldn't blame him for feeling as he did. She'd been there herself once or twice a long, long time ago.

Julia brought the car to a stop at the end of Exmouth Street where the pavement ended and the gravel surface took over. About a **hundred** yards farther along, the gravel gave way to the St. Clair River and an old, rusted, mostly buried hulk of a long-since scuttled barge—she had followed him here once. Since that time, she had found him sitting atop that barge beyond the No Trespassing signs on three other occasions.

Her heart broke to see him staring across the river toward the States. He looked so lost and alone, but she couldn't let him see her pity. He wouldn't respond to pity. After all, he prided himself as a tough guy.

She left the car where the paved surfaced ended and walked to the twelve-foot fence cordoning off the area from trespassers. She didn't notice the black limousine creeping up behind her next to her car.

Reaching up, she took a hold of the fence. Allowing the yielding links to take her weight, she leaned into it. "Been here all night?

At first, he appeared startled, but quickly regained his cool. "What's it to you?" he quipped.

"Must have been hellish cold out here last night."

"Yeah, so what!" he spat back.

"Have you eaten? Are you hungry?" she offered.

"Sure, I've eaten. Shit sakes, lady. They got five-star dining on this here tub!" His tone was no softer. "Hey lady, get the hell away from me. Why do you keep coming around for, anyway? Can't you find nobody your own age?"

"Yeah, sure I can, but they're all afraid of me. Not like you though, right? You're not afraid of anything, are you?"

"Bet your ass."

"Sure, that's why you're always hiding out down here."

"Yeah, so what!"

"Hey listen, I'd love to stand here all day long and let you shoot sunshine up your own ass. But I'm cold and I'm going to get something to eat. If you want to join me, get your ass into my car and we'll go. If not, you can sit up there until you freeze your balls off." A momentary look of shock crossed his face. This was a side of her he had never seen before... he liked it..

Julia turned and started back toward her car. The limousine was nowhere in sight. Minutes passed before she heard the sound of Tom running up behind her. "Hey lady, where'd you learn to talk like that?"

"What's it to you? Get in."

After filling his stomach, Julia delivered him to school so he could finish out the day. That done, she headed toward his mother's house to inform her that he was all right and no harm had been done. However, when she arrived at the home she found no one there. For an instant her enthusiasm, so intense earlier that same day, was slipping. It was no wonder Tom behaved as he did. The woman didn't work, yet she couldn't stay at home long enough to make sure her only child was safe. Oh, there would be a rash of seemingly legitimate excuses as to why she had to leave the house without knowing of her son's well-being. But none of them would even come close to the truth. It was becoming more and more difficult for Julia to entertain leaving this "family"— the term used loosely— together.

It was well after one p.m. when she finally managed to return to the office. Some of the staff were putting up the usual cardboard cut-outs of Santa. His cotton beard was tattered, but none of them looked too concerned over it. Cardboard cut-outs, a few bows and tinsel strung here and there; it all seemed so cheap to her, so completely inadequate.

Without acknowledging those she passed, Julia returned to her desk. She took a seat, folded her hands beneath her chin and closed her eyes.

**"... Hello, little girl. What's your name?" No response ... "Are you lost?" At this, the small, redheaded child giggled ... Was this some sort of a game? ... Finally, she spoke. "Not me ... I'm not lost ... but you are..."**

"Julia.... Hello, anybody in there?" She returned with a start. Susan was standing in the entrance to her cubicle, looking slightly concerned over Julia's absentmindedness. "'Hey, girl! What's wrong? Are you all right? What happened with Tom Mitchell, anyway?"

"Nothing, everything is fine with him. I think we might have to pull him, though," Julia replied.

"Julia," she began cautiously. "You aren't becoming attached to this one, are you? If you are, you know I'll have to reassign the case."

"So what if I am! The kid's own mother, and I use the term loosely, doesn't give a damn about the boy!" she raged. "Why is it so damned wrong for me to care about him?"

"Care all you like, just don't become emotionally involved," Susan warned.

"You make it sound so simple."

"'Listen, I know how hard it is not to take each of these kids back home with you at the end of the day, Julia, but you just can't do it! Besides, it's against regulations, " Susan added.

Julia hated regulations. She hated everything about them. To her, they stood for restrictions, road blocks keeping her from doing what she knew was right. "May I have the rest of the day off? All of a sudden I feel really sick to my stomach."

"Take Monday as well. Perhaps when you return you will be in a frame of mind better suited to do the job you were hired for." Some of the friendliness left Susan's voice. Its absence clearly affirmed she meant ever word.

**Julia stood in the corner of what appeared to be a large attic room watching a bizarre scene being played out before her. Through the warped and rotting floorboards wisps of thick, white smoke curled into the attic. A great need, a feeling of urgency, filled her.... But why? ...what was she even doing here in this room? Then a sight, which until that instant was hidden from her, was revealed. Near the rear wall opposite to the door, she could see herself standing with a small child at her right side.... No way ... not possible! I can't be in two places at once! It just isn't possible. Not possible and yet it was happening. A sensation so strange descended around her. A feeling of dire concern for the safety of those before her and yet at the same time a distance that was almost comforting .... Something was happening now ....**

**Her other self took the child in her arms and was carrying her through the smoke-filled room toward the door. Through the smoke haze the child turned to Julia and, smiling, said, "Julia... remember."**

"Son-of-a-bitch! What the hell was that?" she demanded aloud, sitting bolt upright and feeling uneasy in the darkness of her room. Reaching over, she turned on the bedside lamp, dispelling the ghosts she felt were so very near. She sat staring through bewildered, distant eyes.

She knew about dreams and what brought them about. Her psychology training had given her that much. However, this dream was different. It had been strangely haunting and, for reasons she could not explain, seemed more of a remembrance of events past. She knew this was completely impossible. She had never been in such a situation.

It was still terribly earlier, but further sleep was probably out of the question. She got out of bed and made her way through the darkened apartment. The sun would be rising soon. The horizon was already beginning to show signs of the awakening day. Today was Saturday— her time. Today she would not have to deal with the problems of those who didn't care anyway. Today was hers to laze around and put her sanity back in order before the following Tuesday when it would all start again.

On the small table in the hall a stack of mail she couldn't be bothered to read the day before sat waiting for her. Scooping it up, she moved toward the couch and threw herself down. There was the usual assortment of garbage that invariably accompanied the daily deliveries, especially during the Christmas season. Almost as soon as she began to sort through it, the sun rising slowly into another dull winter sky drew her gaze away.

The dreams still haunted her nights. Even the new location hadn't helped as she had hoped it might. The dreams or nightmares or whatever they were didn't frighten her... well, not really. Mostly they just tormented her, tormented her with partial memories—if that was what they were—and vague images of events she knew nothing about. And always she awoke with a single burning question: *remember what?*

# CHAPTER 9

A light drizzle washed the outer panes. The grey sky showed no signs of allowing the sun to show through.

Rows of chairs stood empty. But then, she expected this. The man shut himself off everything before he died, and for that—the emptiness of the room—Delse mourned. It was such a waste that a man should live his entire life only to find no one really cared enough or felt close enough to attend his funeral.

The minister looked uneasy. Clearly, he too was uncomfortable with the lack of mourners to whom he could preach—a congregation of one, his worst ever.

"Miss … Shall I begin?" he asked sheepishly.

"I doubt anyone else will be coming, Father. You may as well," Delse replied, her own emotions locked loosely within.

The service was short and simple before the casket was wheeled into another room to be prepared for cremation.

"Would you like a moment, Miss?" the minister asked.

"No. No, that's all right. You go and do what needs to be done." Delse saw the remorse in his eyes. He seemed almost embarrassed by his concern, and, without another offer of solace, quickly turned and left room.

The drizzle had subsided, if only a little, when Delse finally walked out through the front doors of the funeral home. She didn't feel like going home. There were too many considerations to be taken into account now. What was she to do with the house— should she move in, or sell it? "Maybe a walk along the river would clear your head," she told herself, unintentionally aloud.

Somehow, the waterfront didn't look quite as beautiful as it had the other night. It was strange how the light of day could so easily steal away its magic. Exposed wires and black extension cords, hidden by night, ran prominently in all directions.

Moving to the railing, she stared out over the river. The water was dark, angry, churned by unseen hands. Atop the Blue Water Bridge, hazard lights flashing upon its tallest span drew her eyes and held them there. A steady stream of traffic travelling in both directions crowded the concrete surface below.

"How come you look so sad?" asked the sweet voice of a small girl. Delse hadn't heard her come up.

"Huh? Are you talking to me?" Delse asked softly.

"Nobody else here."

"No, I guess you're right."

"Well, how come?"

"My daddy died. That's why I'm so sad."

"I'm sorry." She was a pretty little girl with a slender face and long crimped red hair; she was undoubtedly destined to break a lot of hearts once she grew up.

"What's your name?" Delse asked.

"Mickey. My name is Mickey!" she proclaimed proudly.

"Well, Mickey. What are you doing down here all by yourself? Where are your parents?" Delse asked, scanning the paths for them.

"I don't know. But that's okay, I'm not alone. You're here now."

"I think maybe we should go and try to find them. What do you say?" Delse suggested. Mickey shrugged her tiny shoulders and took Delse's hand.

They completed the circuit around the park with no sign of Mickey's parents.

"Are you sure they're …" Delse stopped mid-sentence. Mickey was gone. "Huh?" Delse gasped, an uneasy feeling creeping along her spine. "What the hell is going on?" She searched the plywood scenes to see if perhaps Mickey was hiding behind one of them. Her eyes fell upon a depiction of the birth of Christ. Not the entire scene, only the little whitewashed angel attached in the gable of the miniature stable. Its slender, downcast face and flowing tresses resembled those of the small girl with whom Delse had spent the last hour.

On the street behind her she became aware of movement. She turned to investigate and saw the large black limousine rolling slowly along the curb. Her eyes shot wide. Her pulse raced.

"Better run, Delse. He's coming for you!" Mickey's whispery voice came floating through the air, though she was nowhere in sight.

Delse didn't understand. "What's happening?" she demanded. This time, Mickey didn't respond. Delse fell into a dead run.

Centennial Park didn't offer much cover; only large rolling hills at the end of the path.

Delse wasted no time getting to them. Still, the limousine followed. Hidden now from the road behind the hills, Delse slowed her pace. Her mind reeled, searching for a route of escape. There were no alleys here.

A small playground came into view. It wasn't much more than a slide and a swing set. A small child swung slowly, scraping her feet in the muddy ground. It was Mickey. Delse watched as Mickey swayed back and forth on the swing. Then, all at once, she was gone.

Vanished.

"Ah shit …. This is too weird!" Delse said, confused.

"Don't stop … they're still coming." Again Mickey's voice floated through the air.

Not knowing which she feared more, the voice or the limousine, Delse broke into a run across the park toward a motel some seventy-five yards away. The high heels she wore hindered every stride. Each breath screamed from her lungs. The result of far too many cigarettes, she told herself.

She was almost to the motel. Only a small dock stood between her and her safety—twenty yards, no more than that. Someone was sitting on the dock. It was the small girl again!

"They're gone now …. You can stop running," Mickey said.

"What?" Delse gasped, trying to regain her breath. "Who are you?" she demanded,

"I told you, I'm Mickey. Don't you remember?" the little girl said.

Delse glanced back across the park to make sure she wasn't still being followed. Satisfied it was now safe, she turned back to the little girl, only to find her gone again. Delse's legs felt weak. Her vision clouded until all that remained were murky shades of grey.

Desperately, her mind clung to consciousness. It was to no avail— blackness overtook.

# CHAPTER 10

The road was almost completely void of homes. To her right a huge, three-storey house... her next stop. Its blacked-out windows and charred roof were somehow familiar to her and somehow soothing under the dark-grey storm clouds threatening to do their worst overhead. Her mail bag weighty with the many Christmas flyers, she started toward the structure. A small redheaded girl stood a short distance away beneath an old, lightning-struck tree.

"Hello, Meagan," she said.

"Do I know you?" Meagan replied. The child only giggled. Her voice had an echo to it, as though they were in a large empty room.

"What do you want? Who are you?" Meagan demanded.

"They're waiting in there for you. I wouldn't go in there if I were you. He'll get you if you do."

Rusty patches of snow dotted the ditches along Highway Four south-bound. The sky, though threatening snow earlier in the day, was now showing a more pleasant side of its personality. The sun pouring through the wind shield warmed her face. Next to her, behind the wheel, sat Bruce. It was his idea to drive to Sarnia and actually visit the remains of the orphanage located just outside a much smaller town called Petrolia. Meagan pushed herself into an upright position. "How much longer?" she asked, still heavy from sleep.

"We just went through Hanover .... I'd say an hour, perhaps two."

"Great. My butt's asleep," she complained.

"Do you want me to stop the car so you can stretch your legs?"

"No, I'm fine."

"Suit yourself."

There was a brief silence between them. Then Meagan asked, "Bruce do you think we are doing the right thing?"

"What, by going to see the place? I can't see any harm coming from it, if that's what you mean. Why do you ask?"

"I don't really know. I'm just getting a strange feeling about all of this."

"You're just nervous. You're about to find part of what you've been searching for, and you are not really sure you want it anymore."

"You some kind of shrink or something?"

"Or something."

"Yeah, well, stick to what you know."

"Everybody's a critic," he sighed and turned on the car's radio. The local country station was tuned in. Meagan flipped through the stations before turning it off again. "Hey!" he protested. "Don't you like 'hurtin'-truck-drivin'-wife-losing' tunes?"

"No, why do you?"

"Kinda."

"You're such a loser," she teased.

Without the aid of the radio to break the monotony, the time passed slowly. Conversation dwindled and before too much longer Meagan was asleep again. He had never known a woman who could sleep so much.

> Before her now was a large, red-brick apartment complex.... number 4856 Ashborne ... Why was she here? Was there someone here? .... Inside now ... The apartment door says 304. Who lives here?
>
> "Go inside. She's a really nice lady. You'll like her," the little girl with red hair insisted.
>
> "Who are you?" Meagan asked.
>
> "Delse knows."
>
> "Who's Delse?" Meagan asked.
>
> "She lives here…"

"Asshole! Keep your eyes on the God-damned road!" Bruce shouted out the window. His words were useless. The offender was long gone in the opposite direction.

"What's going on?" Meagan demanded, still only half awake.

"Didn't you see that moron? He came right into my lane. Hell, I almost had to ditch it to avoid him!"

"Maybe you should let me drive for a while," she offered.

"Don't worry about it. I'm fine," he grumbled.

"Okay, fine. Don't eat me." She turned her attention toward the passing fields. Her mind was distant, troubled. Something was waiting for them. She was almost sure of it now … but what?

# CHAPTER 11

The furniture now gone, and there were yards of urine-stained carpet piled on the front porch. Delse stood in the living room of what once was her father's house. Now it was hers, hers to do as she liked. She would sell. There were too many memories—bad memories—for her here. However, before it went on the market it was going to need a lot of fixing up.

Vast white drop cloths were draped across the battered hardwood floor. Sending her roller home into the pan she brought forth a full load of paint and turned toward the wall. It went on thick and pure, hiding the years of neglect beneath a pristine coat of white.

An hour and a half later the room was completed. The smell of the fresh paint permeated her nostrils. White paint spatterings freckled every inch of exposed skin, and with it came a sense of loss, or perhaps guilt. It needed to be done, yet the sense that she was desecrating a shrine was inescapable. Would he have approved? she wondered... probably not, but it didn't matter anymore. She set the roller down and walked into the kitchen. Several cardboard cartons awaited their allotment of dishes still inhabiting the time- yellowed cupboards.

Trance-like at first, she began the task of loading the boxes. Soon the shelves visible from the floor were empty. Only the top shelf remained. In all the years she lived in this house, never once did she see what occupied that shelf. Perhaps it never seemed important enough to investigate. Mounting a small step ladder, left for this very reason, she peered onto the top shelf. It was empty except for a large, grease-stained yellow envelope.

Descending to the floor, holding the envelope at arm's length, she stared vacantly at its metal butterfly closure.

Inside were several black and white photographs. She could only guess who the people were … her real parents, perhaps. They looked young, and were probably not married. A date was printed in ink on the back of each picture, but nothing to tell her their names. The fourth picture was of a house. A large old house set far back from the road. It was the same one she dreamt about. Any other time she might have dismissed the similarity as coincidence, but in the wake of all that had happened to her recently she could not. In the foreground of the shot there was a sign and its lettering was clear. It dispelled any doubts she might have had.

## FORGIVING HEARTS ORPHANAGE
## "BLESSED BE THOSE OF FORGIVING HEARTS"

"Why," she wondered aloud. "Why is this happening to me now? After all these years, why now?"

None of it made sense: The dreams of the house in the picture; the man in the grey trench coat who seemed to know her every move; the little girl in the park. What did it all mean? She couldn't begin to figure it out. She didn't even know where to start. Perhaps her real parents were psychics... she dismissed the possibility of that as quickly as it occurred to her. No, there had to be some reason, some physical explanation for all of this. Though, if one existed, it was hidden from her.

A chill ran along her spine as she returned the pictures to the envelope and folded the flap shut.

The house was still and eerie, so the click of the front door latch resounded like a shotgun blast.

Snapped out of her imaginings, Delse turned to investigate, only to find the guy in the wool coat striding toward her through the now-empty living and dining rooms.

Another click from behind. Frantically, she scanned the room for anything to use as a weapon. Her hand found a 26-ounce rum bottle. Without a moment's hesitation, she smashed it against the counter, bringing it up rapidly and slashing wildly at her assailant's face. He evaded her easily enough.

Arms wide, he seemed to be baiting her, drawing her attention away from the back of the house.

Too late, she realized what he was doing. She had forgotten about the threat from the rear. A powerful hand clamped over her face. The acrid odour of chloroform invaded her nasal passage. Instinct took over as she savagely stabbed the offending arm with the jagged glass.

"Fuck!" he roared. "Take this bitch, will you?"

The one in the wool coat stepped forward.

Grey mist was now descending, followed by inky blackness threatening to engulf her. Her futile attempts to defend herself ended as the remnants of the bottle fell from her lifeless hand.

# CHAPTER 12

Bruce eased the car onto the shoulder next to the entrance of the driveway. On the opposite side of the road was a small farmhouse set back from the road. A mailbox labelled LEAP marked the driveway.

The historical society had given him the directions and now here they were staring at the distant charred remains of the Forgiving Heart Orphanage.

The roof was gone. The outer walls, their blackened empty windows daring all comers, remained intact.

The weather-faded sign near the road hung precariously from a single hinge. It swayed awkwardly in the winter wind sweeping across the snow-covered fields.

The snow between the road and the ancient structure lay undisturbed. No one had been here in a very long time.

A chill rocked Meagan's body. What best-forgotten memories awaited her here? The urge to leave was enormous. However, the desire to stay was even greater. She got out of the car and stood on the shoulder of the road.

"Ready?" Bruce asked, sounding uncertain.

"May as well. We're here now." Without waiting for him to walk around the car, she started through the ditch.

Nothing before her now was familiar, and yet in some strange way, she knew it all well. Visions flashed through her mind; visions of the house in its former array. With them came an image of other children. Little girls, perhaps friends, and this comforted her. Somehow just knowing she hadn't been alone living in this brooding structure made her feel better. However, along with the comfort was something else, something dark … something frightening. Where were they now? she wondered.

"Be careful of the floor. It could be rotten after all of this time," Bruce cautioned as she mounted the stairs and moved toward the blackened doorframe.

The entrance opened into a large kitchen, typical of the era when the house was first built. The ceiling was gone all the way up to the third floor. A barrage of nesting birds took flight as they entered.

Three doors led from this room to other parts of the house. One lead to a stairway once leading to the second floor; however, the fire had reduced the steps to blackened cinders clinging to the exterior brick. The second one led to the main living quarters of the house, where sections of the ceiling still clung precariously to ancient moorings. The third led to the cellar, but the way was blocked by massive collapsed support beams.

"Are you getting anything from this?" Bruce asked, keeping a watchful eye for possible hazards. There was certainly no shortage of them.

"Little bits; it feels weird, but that's about it. I'm ready to go now, if you are."

"Let's go, then."

Turning to follow him out, Meagan was distracted by the faint sound of a child giggling. Knowing it was impossible, she went to investigate the source anyway. There was no child— only a long-forgotten ragdoll tossed carelessly into a corner of one of the smaller adjacent rooms. She picked it up.

*"Remember me?"* floated past Meagan's ear like a breeze.

"Meagan, come on," Bruce called from the side porch. "We should be heading back to the hotel. It's getting late"

"I'm coming, I'm coming," she insisted, appearing immediately in the doorway. "Look what I found."

"A kid's doll, so what. It was probably left in there by kids using this place as a playhouse."

"I don't think so. Look, part of the dress is singed. It must have belonged to someone living here before the fire."

"Even if you're right, it still doesn't tell us anything."

"What did you hope to accomplish by bringing me out here, anyway?" she asked.

"I don't know. I thought bringing you here would help you remember something."

"Sorry, there's nothing," she said. She was lying. Well, not really. What she remembered were feelings, vague fleeting images all coming together so strangely nothing could be easily explained. She would keep it to herself a while longer, at least until she was sure.

# CHAPTER 13

The day was dragging. It was filled with the usual assortment of irate parents, intolerable children and hopeful adoptees. There seemed no end to the needs and concerns of those streaming through her office that afternoon. Still, determined to do her job as pleasantly as possible, Julia fought to keep the smile glued to her face.

The last of her scheduled appointments left the office at four-fifteen. Julia had a headache like none other she had ever known. She closed her eyes, leaned back in her chair and gently rubbed the bridge of her nose.

"Busy lady," Susan observed, poking her head into Julia's cubicle. "How'd the day go?"

"Susan, tell me something. Why the hell do these people bother having kids in the first place? It boggles my mind," she whined. "For example, there was a young couple in here this afternoon. They wanted to adopt a child, any child. It didn't matter to them if the child was black, white or green, for Christ sake. They just wanted someone to share their love with and what did I do for them? I'll tell you what I did for them. I put their names on an eight-year waiting list just so they can go on another list when the first eight years is up. I thought they were going to cry when they left here. Then, not five minutes later a woman storms in here dragging her bratty kid. Neither has a kind word for the other. He says he can't stand her. She says she wishes he was never born and demands he be placed in Huron House! Why do people do it?"

"I hear you. People who could offer a wonderful home for a child can't have them, while morons who have no business becoming parents have dozens. Go figure. It's called reality. Get used it, because it sure as hell doesn't get any better."

"Thanks, Sue. You really cheered me up with that. "

"Anytime." Susan was about to leave when the reason she appeared in the first place returned to her. "Oh yeah, I almost forgot. A bunch of us are going for a drink after work. Want to join us? After all, it is Friday night."

"After the day I've had you can definitely count me in!"

"Good, see you in a bit."

Two men milling about the parked cars tried to look as though they belonged while waiting for Julia to leave the building. In a few short minutes, this phase of the assignment would be over and they could move on to the next.

The outer office doors opened and out stepped Julia accompanied by four of her colleagues. "Are we all taking our own cars?" one of them asked.

"Yeah, I'd rather not have to take a taxi down here in the morning to get it," Susan said.

The man standing closest to Julia's car moved quietly away.

He hadn't expected this. There were too many witnesses to carry out his orders cleanly. It would have to wait. A better opportunity was sure to present itself.

Both men met back at the car a short while later. They would deliver their present cargo before returning for the blonde.

Huddled in one corner of the back seat, her mouth gagged and her hands and feet bound tightly, was Delse.

"For Christ's sake, the little witch got the hood off again!"

"Well, fix it and let's get the hell out of here."

Moments later the limousine pulled into the street and headed for the highway.

\*\*\*

A temperate winter's breeze brought on by an approaching storm carried the essence of thawing soil to Julia's senses.

After a few drinks, the tensions of the past week eased their grip. Still, her preoccupation was too complete to relax and enjoy the outing. Having left the others at the bar, she started for home. Thinking better than to try driving, she had opted to walk. It wasn't a great distance and a chance of getting caught in the storm was too hard to pass up. She loved storms. Though she was aware it probably represented some psychological malady, their violence calmed her.

Sheet lightning flashed in the sky. What had been only a slight breeze moments before was now a formidable wind. It tossed her hair, pulling it away from her face only to throw it forward again. It felt wondrous. With each buffeting assault, she could feel her concerns lessening, and before long she was free of them. Nothing else existed, only her, the wind and soon the driving rain.

"Better hurry along, Miss. You're gonna catch your death," warned a kind-looking old man from his front porch as Julia walked past. She smiled, waved and walked on.

Sarnia, though numbering some eighty thousand since the amalgamation between the city and township, was essentially a small town. As their surroundings grew, the people here didn't lose their smiles and mostly could still be trusted. She couldn't remember the last time she passed someone on the street and had not been met with a nod or a smile. It made her feel good inside each time it happened. Oh sure, there were bad elements here as there were everywhere else, but too few to take notice of. Because of this, she felt no apprehension when two men approached from the opposite direction.

There was an old standing joke about Sarnia men that said for those born in Sarnia the standard mode of dress was a baseball cap, blue jeans and a sweatshirt.

By this standard, the two approaching were definite imports to the region. They wore suits and heavy woollen overcoats that looked out of place considering the lateness of the hour. Their appearance noted, she prepared a smile. The gap lessened, and as they passed the friendliness Julia looked forward to didn't materialize. Instead, her smile met with a harsh butt from a solid shoulder as the man on the left refused to yield.

"And a good evening to you too," she murmured in disgust.

All at once a powerful hand clasped across her face. Her eyes began to water. A sharp odour flooded her senses. The hand tightened. Her weakening attempts to remove it were to no avail. The street lights overhead became fuzzy before fading out altogether.

# CHAPTER 14

Meagan sat across the breakfast table staring distantly through the smoked glass window of the hotel cafe. What would their next move be?? Nothing she could share had come from their visit to the orphanage. And there were no records to suggest a possible direction for their investigation to take. Unquestionably, their search was beginning to look more and more like a hopeless wild goose chase.

"We should head on back to Collingwood. After all, we're not going to find what we're looking for by sitting here," she sighed.

As much as Bruce hated to admit to it, she was right. The investigation had come to a full stop, a dead end.

"Your adopted parents don't have any idea as to who your real parents were?" It was a basic question. Yet somehow he hadn't thought to ask it until now.

"Oh, sure, probably, but they don't agree with this little quest of ours. They as much as told me they would never help me with it."

"I think maybe you're right. It is time we headed for home, but only for a day or two." There was a tone in his voice that she found intriguing. It left her wanting more, but more was not forthcoming. "Come on, let's get our stuff."

While he spoke, an idea occurred to her. "You go ahead. There's something I want to check into first," Meagan said.

"Hey, I thought I was the constable," Bruce protested.

"Don't worry ... you'll still get paid," she teased. "Meet me back here in an hour." With that, she was gone.

The dream she'd had during the drive from Collingwood to Sarnia haunted her. So she was a bit shocked when she gave the driver the address and he didn't as much as blink. Could it possibly be an actual address? Could whoever this Delse Collier was be a real person and not just a product of her fevered imagination? She was about to find out.

The taxi slowed to a stop in front of a red brick apartment building. It looked just as it did in her dream. For a moment, she sat there in the back seat of the cab and stared blankly, marvelling over the similarities.

"I'll be right back. Wait for me here," Meagan told the driver before leaving the cab and walking into the building.

There was an old register posted on one wall of the small lobby. She scanned the numbers. Soon her finger found number 304 and moved across to the name "D. Collier." Having come this far into the absurd, Meagan decided to follow it through to the end. She pushed the button that would summon D. Collier in unit 304.

Meagan pushed the button for a second time and now a feeling of complete lunacy fell upon her. What she was doing and why she was even here in the first place was the result of a dream. How could she explain this without this D. Collier calling the cops and having her locked up? Why did she even care?

Feeling more and more ridiculous as the seconds passed, Meagan left the lobby and returned to the safe, sane harbour of the taxi.

"Where to now, Miss?" the driver asked.

"Back to the hotel, please, and could you hurry? This place gives me the creeps."

Meagan and Bruce were packed and on the highway headed out of Sarnia within the hour. Silence enveloped them as they passed over the town's outer limits.

Hope … faith … these things made up a large portion of who Meagan was inside. To lose either of them now would be disastrous. Steeling herself against an onslaught of self-pity, she gazed out the open car window searching for anything to take her mind from her worries.

Coming to Sarnia and actually seeing the orphanage had become such a vast source of hope. Now it was all she could do to keep it from caving in on itself.

Bruce could see it in her eyes. She was about to give up. He couldn't allow that to happen— not yet, anyway. He had a plan. There was one last chance of finding the lead they so desperately needed in order to continue.

Somewhere along the line he had lost his professional emotional detachment and now found himself resenting Tina and Craig Bathurst. After all, what right did they have to deny Meagan this? None, where he was concerned.

His plan was simple. He would wait until the Bathursts were not at home, then break in and find the documentation his client needed. Unethical, perhaps, but ethics and reason soon lose their lustre when emotions come into play. And his emotions were fully involved. Now his only concern was to see Meagan happy. If only he knew what happiness meant for her.

Sudden movement in the rear-view mirror drew his eye as a pale-green Dodge Dart roared up from behind. He watched it closely. The driver's actions were wildly erratic. Seconds later, the driver of the Dart took the car across the centre line and gunned the accelerator. Not wanting to appear antagonistic, Bruce removed his foot from the gas pedal to allow the other car to pass. To his surprise, it did not. Instead, it held a solid position next to them. The other car matched their speed exactly.

The man on the passenger side of the Dart motioned wildly for Bruce to roll down his window.

"What the hell!" Meagan exclaimed.

There was no response. Bruce was too busy trying to keep the car between the ditches.

He rolled down his window.

Suddenly, a slight whiff of smoke could be seen in the cabin of the other car. A hot stinging sensation flared at the base of Bruce's skull.

"Meagan, take the wheel!" he commanded.

"What!"

"Do it! I think I've been shot!"

Unsure of herself, Meagan did as she was told. He was losing consciousness rapidly, though there was no sign of blood. His right foot grew heavy upon the accelerator. The seconds elapsed, taking consciousness further and further out of his reach. The car lurched forward. Its speed increased until it was out of all control. Meagan struggled desperately to dislodge his foot from the pedal. It was all so hopeless. She needed both of her hands on the wheel.

The brake! The thought struck her like a cold fist. It was her last chance. Her body still confined by the seat belt, which was twisted awkwardly, she stomped the brake with all the force she could summon. The car veered wildly, and at first showed no sign of slowing.

Somehow, in the struggle to regain control, the car leapt across the centre line and now found itself in the direct path of an oncoming transport. The truck's horn filled the air with urgent blasts. Its huge brakes strained against its incredible bulk. The distance between them evaporated at an unreal pace. Meagan bore down hard to the left. The car struck the shoulder like an out-of-control rocket and within that split second went airborne. Nothing remained to be done. "Hang on!" she screamed as though he could hear her. The car soared as though in slow motion and all at once the flight ended with an abrupt thud. The front end of the car was partially buried, its rear wheels still spinning, but the ordeal appeared to have ended.

Meagan was wrong.

# CHAPTER 15

"Are they still alive?" asked Stanley Kwik. He was a nervous man who fidgeted constantly, not at all suited for his tasks of late. When his cousin had summoned him from England five and a half months earlier there was no mention of a kidnapping. Still, he would go along with it. Meacha would be angry if he did not. He knew beyond a doubt she would return him to England to face the attempted murder charges against him. It was a wonder she could get him out in the first place— when asked about it, Meacha would say only that she was able to pull a few strings ... nothing more.

"Idiot! Of course they are," scolded a much larger man engaged in examining the three women. "Tell Meacha I'll be down in a few moments."

His name was Fred Dressel—Doctor Fred Dressel. At least, he was before his licence was revoked three years earlier.

He was an imposing man standing six-feet, four-inches tall. His hair, peppered with grey, receded at the temples toward the crown of his head, leaving only a tuft over his forehead, worn long and combed straight back. His stern manner and sheer size were enough to make anyone think twice before confronting him. It was a trait he had used to his advantage often.

One quick last look and Dressel picked up a small metal tray and closed and locked the door before going to speak with Meacha. He found her in the den; a room closed off from the others by huge sliding oak doors. When the doors were all opened a huge wheel-shaped ballroom formed. Though many years had passed since the space was actually used for that purpose.

Her back was to the door as he entered the room "How are my guests?" she asked without turning to acknowledge him there.

"They're fine, Meacha. The anesthetic is keeping them under very nicely. I suspect we could keep them out for two, perhaps three, more days," Dressel said, moving to mix himself a drink.

"…and the samples I requested?"

"I have them here."

Meacha had turned and now watched him closely in his liberties.

"Dressel, I don't recall offering you a drink." Her words were lightly spoken, though their razor edge was unmistakeable. "Put it down. You would do well to remember just whose house this is."

"Yes, Meacha, my apologies," he cowed.

"That's much better," she said, accepting his submission. She moved toward him and took him lightly by the arm. "I feel my guests have slept long enough. Don't you agree?" she said, expecting no opposition, and none came. "You will discontinue the dosage effective immediately."

"Yes, Meacha."

"Very well, go inform the others of my decision," she said, smiling as she walked him to the door as though seeing off an old friend.

Turning back into the room, she stood staring at a large oil painting mounted on the far wall.

"Don't worry dear … soon."

# CHAPTER 16

**Whispers of feathery mist danced and swirled about the sparse stand of pine that was so faint, yet retarding images only a few metres distant. All around loomed ghost-like hulks reaching in fruitless attempts to capture. Ahead, not more than twenty metres, a muffled glow beckoned.**

**There was no fear of the unexpected, the unexplained. Shafts of pure light leapt from the child, reaching out to each of them encompassing all present in its shimmering embrace. Warmth like none they had ever known spread over them. It filled their hearts, freeing their minds of the walls constructed over a lifetime of pain and resentment.**

The door closed softly, followed by the rattle of keys in the lock.

Opening one heavy eyelid, a vestige of frills, of lace and of satin flooded inward. The room was immense though sparsely furnished. What furnishings there were looked antique and polished to a high gloss. However, upon the room's present occupant their wonders were wasted. Delse was not impressed by the austere décor. Nothing lived here. Everything was in its place…too much so. There was no dust, not the slightest hint anywhere. Each piece was a perfect complement to everything else in the room. *Too perfect*, she thought, pushing herself to the edge of the cot.

There were two other military-style cots similar to hers and on them were two other women. Both were still unconscious. Strangely, a smile briefly passed across Delse's face. Maybe it was because she was no longer alone in whatever this was. Perhaps it was the obvious blunder the interior decorator had made by adding the three canvas cots to the room. But with that, there was something else. Something about the cots tugged at the edges of memory. Why did she think there should be one more?

Her arm ached from the needle her abductors had used to drug her. A nasty-looking bruise discoloured the skin. There was a sick feeling in her stomach and a slight taste of garlic on her tongue.

"Wonderful, first I'm kidnapped then forced to eat garlic," she quipped, realizing the taste was a probable side effect from the drug.

She didn't belong here. There was no question. The others would feel the same once they awoke. Understandably out of place amidst such frivolous things, she stood upon uncertain legs and moved about the room. "What is this place?" she demanded silently. There came no reply.

Two windows overlooked the extensive grounds. They were obviously well tended, but offered nothing that might tell her who was responsible for the abduction.

On the floor inside the door were three trays of food covered with metal lids. Steam rose from each of them. At the foot of each of the three cots was a neatly folded change of clothes. Delse was prepared to lay odds they'd be a perfect fit.

There was movement now from others as the first waves of reviving teased their unconscious minds. Delse sat on the edge of her cot and watched, waiting for the drug to lose its grip completely.

"How's it going?" Delse asked as one of the women lifted her head from the canvas.

At first there came no response. The woman was obviously startled at finding herself here. Soon she found her tongue. "What the hell is going on here!" Julia demanded. "How did I get here?"

"Don't ask me," Delse began. "Though I'm pretty sure we all arrived the same way."

"Yeah, unconscious," Meagan muttered, lifting her head.

"Who would do such a thing?" Julia seemed dumbstruck.

"Beats the hell out of me. Whoever they are, they want us well fed and in clean clothes," Delse said, bringing their attention to the clothes and the trays of food.

"Who could eat?" Meagan grumbled. Her muscles were stiff from the crash. "I think I'm going to puke. What'd they knock us out with, anyway?"

"Who knows? But whatever it was and whatever they're after, it would appear the three of us are somehow involved. We might as well get to know each other. I'm Delse Collier."

"Meagan Bathurst. I wish I knew what the hell was going on. Where's Bruce?" she said, making no effort at pleasantry.

"I'm Julia Hart. Bruce?"

"Yes, he was driving when we were run off the road. He said he had been shot. I tried to take the wheel, but we lost control … last thing I remember was the car flipping over."

"Maybe he's in another room?" Delse offered.

"I think it would be a good idea if we were to look for something in common that could tie each of us together. Maybe we can figure this out," Julia said.

Delse nodded agreement, thinking, *Didn't I just say that?*

Meagan sat staring distantly at the wall, her brow furrowed. Something monstrous and elusive swam through her murky mind. Julia was the first to notice.

"Meagan, what is it?"

Meagan turned silently toward them, not saying anything for a moment, as if gathering her thoughts. "This is going to sound crazy… but while we were driving down here to Sarnia I fell asleep and dreamt of a little girl with red hair…"

Delse's eyes widened before she blurted out, "Didn't she tell you her name?"

Julia turned to Delse incredulously. It seemed a strange question to ask.

"Yes, it was Mickey, but that's not all. I dreamt that she took me to see you, Delse. She even told me your name! Hell, I took a cab to your apartment yesterday to see if you were real, but there was no answer when I buzzed."

"Yeah, well, I was kinda tied up."

"This is getting stranger by the minute," Julia began.

"You've seen her too, haven't you?" Delse broke in.

"Yes, I have."

"Thank God! I thought I was losing it," Delse sighed

"Well, that might not be all together wrong either," Julia said.

"Thanks a lot." *Bitch*, Delse thought.

"Who is she? Do either of you know?" Meagan asked.

Julia shook her head. "The dreams started a couple weeks ago about the same time as…"

"Someone started following you," Delse said.

---

"Yes."

All at once, a vacant stare cloaked their faces. Each of them had been followed by the same black car, had shared similar dreams of the same little girl and now they had all been abducted. What it all added up to, none was certain. However, it looked as though they were about to find out.

From the hall, beyond the door of their stylish cell, the stirring of heavy feet could be heard. A moment later a key was in the lock. Their hearts were in their throats as the door opened and clean-shaven man with slicked-back blonde hair and sharp features poked his head inside. He seemed surprised to see them revived, but quickly recovered.

"Ah, you are awake. Excellent; someone will be along shortly to collect you. Please be ready." The accent was British, though obviously not borne of breeding. His voice carried traces of his Cockney upbringing, betraying the air he tried so hard to profess.

He was about to leave. Meagan froze him where he stood. "Hey, hold it right there! We demand to know why we've been brought here against our will!" she said, rising swiftly to her feet. She ignored the stiffness and pain in her right side in their attempts to slow her movements. Clearly, she had sustained more injuries in the crash than she had initially realized.

"Unfortunately, Madame, I am not at liberty to say. You will be informed; all in good time. Now, please make yourself ready. You will be collected shortly."

The door closed and locked, and as suddenly as he had first appeared, was gone.

Lacking a better plan of action, they did as they had been instructed. Fifteen minutes later the key was once again in the lock. When the door opened this time, two well-muscled men stepped into the room and stood on either side of the door.

You will come with us," one of them said. At this point, a third, much-smaller man appeared and indicated the direction they were to take.

Each of them rose to their feet. Their backs erect, muscles held taunt, prepared to do battle with whatever or whoever waited beyond the door.

Delse paused briefly and glanced back into the room.

"There should be four," she said softly.

# CHAPTER 17

Nurses in starched white gowns streamed in and out of the room. Until only moments earlier, he had still not regained enough consciousness to object to their continual prodding.

The events of the night before returned slowly. The crash: yes, the accident. Bruce lay heavily bandaged in the St. Joseph Hospital emergency room. Parts of what had happened were clear, but most of it was still fuzzy.

"Hello, Mr. Stewart, good to have you back among the living," said a plump nurse who seemed to suddenly take issue with the position of his pillow and moved to adjust it.

"It doesn't feel so good to be back," he grumbled.

"Now, now, the discomfort you're experiencing will pass."

"I was in a car accident," he began.

"Yes, that's right. How much of it do you remember?"

"Bits and pieces. I remember Meagan was sitting beside me. Then there was the other car. They shot me in the neck with something. I blacked out after that."

"Well, if what you say is true, it would certainly explain the toxicology report."

"Of course it's true! Where's Meagan?"

"Meagan?"

"Yes, Meagan Bathurst. She was in the car with me."

"Sorry, sir, but no one else was found at the crash site. Are you sure she was with you? After all, there was a powerful narcotic in your bloodstream at the time of the crash."

"Of course I'm sure! What kind of ..."

At that moment, the door opened and in walked two men. By the way he was dressed, one was obviously a doctor. The other, Bruce assumed was a cop.

"That will be all, nurse. You may leave now. I'll call you if I need anything further," the doctor instructed before turning his attention to Bruce. "My name is Dr. Jason Corbson, and this is Constable David Thorn. How are you feeling, Mr. Stewart?" The tone of Corbson's voice annoyed him. It sounded limp-wristed.

"I feel like shit."

"Good, shall I take that as a positive sign?"

"You can take it and shove it up your ass, for all I care! What happened to the woman who was travelling with me?"

"There was someone else travelling with you at the time of the crash, sir?" Thorn asked.

"That's what I've been trying to tell you people."

"But, sir…"

"I know. The nurse told me. There was no sign of anyone else at the scene, but I am telling you I was with Meagan Bathurst."

"All we found were two sets of footprints that didn't tie in."

"They've taken her," Bruce sighed, searching his foggy brain for next steps.

"How do you get to that conclusion?" Thorn asked, obviously not buying much of what Bruce had to say.

"It's like I told the nurse. There was another car. They drugged me."

"Nice trick," Thorn smirked. "How'd they do that if they were in the other car?"

"With a dart gun, you fucking moron!" It had become abundantly clear that he was not making himself understood. He would have to get of this place if was going to be of any help at all to Meagan. "I demand to be released," he said, turning to look at the doctor.

"Mr. Stewart, as your doctor I must strongly advise against it."

"Yes, well, you are not my doctor. Either you get the forms in here or I will just get up and leave."

"Sir, you are making a grave error in judgement. You've only been conscious a short time and have suffered a head trauma."

"Clock's ticking, doc."

Shaking his head in frustration, Corbson left the room. Thorn stood looking at Bruce as though trying to decide if there was anything to his story. Removing a business card from his pocket, he placed it on the tray stand and without another word followed Corbson.

A short while later the plump nurse reappeared with the release papers. Bruce had discovered his clothes in a locker near his bed and was gingerly pulling his sweatshirt over his head, careful of the bandages, when she arrived. There was a strange expression on her face…one resembling a combination of worry and resignation.

"Oh, Christ, not you too!"

"Hey… you've refused medical attention. You can drop dead for all I care, but just remember this. If you end up back in here I will have an enema waiting on ice for you," she snarled half-heartedly before pivoting upon her foam soles and squeaking out of the room.

A storm front had moved into the area during the night and all that was ice packed the day before was now buried under six inches of new snow. How different the city looked, he thought, riding back toward the hotel they had recently checked out of.

"Where are you from?" the driver asked.

Bruce turned to respond to the question. So consumed was he with Meagan's disappearance that he hadn't noticed that the driver was missing both legs from the knee down.

"Collingwood."

"Business or pleasure?" the driver asked, eyeing the bandage on Bruce's head.

"Business …. How did it happen?"

"How'd what happen?" The driver was so accustomed to his disability and no longer viewed it as a handicap, so he didn't know what Bruce was referring to.

"Your legs, what happened?"

"Oh, that … car accident as a kid," he said. "Your turn, what did you run afoul of?" he asked.

"I was run off the road." Bruce decided to stick to the cliff notes version of what had happened. The driver just nodded, focussing on the road. "Doesn't it make driving a taxi a little difficult?"

"Not at all," he replied, referring to the hand control that allowed him to operate both the gas and the brake pedal. "This little baby makes it really simple—pull it back to accelerate, push forward to brake. Simple."

"Well, you sure make it look easy," Bruce said, turning his attention back to the snow-covered hedges lining the street.

Once back at the hotel he paid for his ride and started for the lobby. He really had no idea where to start looking for Meagan. Nor did he understand why anyone would want to kidnap her. As far as he was aware she wasn't involved in anything seedy; and this only left him with more blanks to fill in. It was cold, and his head was starting to hurt again. He would need to lie down for a while before readdressing this problem.

He reached the double glass doors and pulled one side open, and then stopped and turned slightly. The taxi was growing distant. A new layer for white was already falling upon the wet surface of the road.

"Damn it, Meagan, where are you?" he murmured before turning and entering the lobby. The glass door closed slowly behind him, the wind and snow held at bay a while longer.

# CHAPTER 18

Twin doors parted and into the room stepped a stern-looking woman of strong bearing. Out of the corner of her eye she watched them, scrutinizing each of the three young women seated on the sofa awaiting her arrival. She didn't acknowledge their presence. Instead, she walked directly to a large wing-back chair featuring a bold red floral print and made herself comfortable.

A long period of heavy silence ensued. She counted her words carefully before beginning. Julia watched her movements intently, searching for a crack leading past the woman's well-perfected granite front. None was evident.

Now a steely assessment – a gaze so piercing that Julia and Meagan forced their eyes away. Delse refused to yield. Though much younger and less experience than their silent host, she was prepared to match wits with her. Some might have considered Delse's reaction to the woman's gaze childish impudence. Delse did not. In her mind, she was merely meeting extreme rudeness in kind. She was determined to prevail.

All at once the others present in the room became aware of the campaign being waged between the two. Then, as though fending off an annoying insect, the woman deftly flicked her wrist and the confrontation was ended. No victor declared.

"The three of you are the only surviving residents of the Forgiving Heart Orphanage. It is therefore possible that one of you is my heir. It is equally possible that none of you are and all of this has been for nothing. In determining which is, in fact, the case, each of you will be expected to undergo the appropriate tests…"

"Like fuck we will!" Delse spat.

"Who the hell do you think you are?" Meagan added.

The woman didn't respond. Clearly, she felt every justification for what she was doing.

Meagan rose to her feet. "You have us followed. You have your thugs kidnap us; you drug us and now this? Lady, you're nuts if you think I'll be subjected to those tests. We're leaving."

Julia and Delse didn't object. They both rose to their feet and moved toward the door. Meagan made a point of walking around the old woman's chair. The woman's driver moved to a position between them and door. No guns were visible. Julia was unaffected by his gesture. She walked up to him and in her most authoritative tone said, "You can drop us of at my apartment. I feel certain you know where that is." He didn't move.

"Hey, Lurch … unless you want to carry your balls in your shirt pocket, I suggest you do as she says," Delse added. Still, he didn't move. His loyalty to the old woman was unwavering.

Julia turned to confront their host and as she did, she saw Meagan palming a letter opener from the desk behind the old woman's chair. "I demand that you release us." The motive for her words changed the instant she saw Meagan. They had to buy her enough time to follow through with whatever she was planning.

The woman's tone was cold. "You will be permitted to leave this house only after my doctors have completed their tests. You will be compensated generously for your trouble."

Meagan made her move.

All at once she had the woman by the arm and was dragging her to her feet, the letter opener from the desk pointed menacingly at her throat. The driver, still guarding the door, squirmed helplessly as the events unfolded before him.

"We're leaving … right now. Tell your goon to get the hell out of our way." Meagan said.

"Oh, very well, do as she says," she sighed. With that, he left his post at the door and allowed them to pass. Meagan maintained a firm grasp on the woman's arm to ensure no one had a change of heart regarding their departure.

Except for the old woman and the driver, the house now appeared to be empty. And so, upon reaching the front door, Meagan released her hold and shoved the woman harshly back into the house and slammed the door.

Her fall had not yet ended when she barked. "Shut the gate! Release the dogs!" The fall ended with a sprawling thud.

The distant hum of the electronically controlled gate and the barking of approaching dogs prompted the trio into a dead heat toward the road.

Without the defence of winter coats, the wind sent chills racing through their bodies, though that concern was now secondary. The gates were still twenty yards away and the gap was decreasing rapidly. Stealing a backward glance, Delse saw three large Dobermans leap from around the side of the house and take chase.

"Let's move it, ladies, or we're going to be lunch for those mutts!" she cried, urging her legs to greater speed. The dogs were closing in quickly, their excited, determined yelps ringing out.

"I can't do it!" Meagan called out, grasping her side that had been badly bruised in the crash.

"The hell you can't! Julia, help me!" Delse commanded. Each took an arm and dragged Meagan along.

The gate was now only feet away Julia and Delse summoned their strength and launched Meagan through the opening just before it closed completely.

Her safety now assured, their own now suspect, they turned to face the dogs. Fanned out, they were now creeping slowly forward to finish what they had started.

Julia and Delse's backs pressed tightly against the gate as they watched the fanged demons approach. "Got any ideas? Now would be a great time to hear them if you do," Julia said in a hoarse whisper. Delse didn't answer. She was looking for something...anything to use against the dogs. Moments later, she found it. A snow shovel lay practically buried only a few feet from the gate. It wasn't much, but it might buy them some time against the dogs.

"Keep 'em busy," Delse commanded.

"How am I supposed to do that?" Julia protested.

"I don't know, think of something."

Delse eased slowly toward the shovel. One of the dogs, noticing the movement, took a step forward. Its growl became even more menacing. Undaunted, she pressed on. Soon her hand closed around the handle. "Okay, when I give the word you climb over the gate. Got it?" Delse instructed.

"What about you?"

"Don't worry; I'll be right behind you."

Swinging the shovel like a club, Delse lashed out viciously at the closest dog. "Now! Go now!" The blade of the shovel found its make just behind the dog's right ear. The animal's cries filled the winter air. Without a moment's pause, she wound up for another swing.

Julia leaped onto the gate and clambered toward the top. Moments later she too was safely on the other side.

Delse's first victim limped whimpering back toward the house. The fight was gone out of it as it trailed crimson in the snow in its wake. Now two remained, and though they were made cautious by her first assault, their vigil was no less resolute. Once again, they crept forward.

Adrenaline pounding her ears, and she swung again. This time the wind caught the blade of the shovel, sending it harmlessly off course. The dogs were dangerously close now. There was no room for another swing.

All at once the air was filled with a barrage of angry shouts; large pieces of ice flew from behind, pelting the dogs. "Move it, Delse! Get the hell out of there. We'll keep them busy."

The ice still soaring through the gate, Delse dropped the shovel and made a desperate lunge at the wrought iron and climbed as quickly as she could toward the top.

They were safe. At least for the moment, but now they found themselves in the middle of nowhere with no coats, no transportation and a long cold night on its way. They'd have to find shelter. They had to find it soon.

# CHAPTER 19

**Long deep shadows held fast to the walls governing the cavern. Damp sand carpeted the floor, filling the dark with the pungent odour of musk. Distant winds haunted aimlessly the seemingly endless expanse. Each step sank slightly into the sand as he moved cautiously forward. What was this place? he wondered. How did he come to be here? The wind was changing now. With it came the tortured screams of a small child. It spurred his movements. Another voice now – that of an angry man. "What's going on here" he demanded aloud. There was no response. Moving faster now, toward the source, he rounded a bend in the tunnel. His eyes opened widely. His heart racing wildly within his chest …**

The phone ringing on the night stand jarred Bruce from sleep. It was Constable Thorn. He wanted to meet to further discuss the possibility of Bruce being correct about the disappearance of Meagan Bathurst. The call was short. They would meet in the hotel restaurant in one hour.

Forty-five minutes elapsed before Bruce entered the restaurant. He wasn't surprised to see Thorn was already there waiting. Thorn looked different. He had put on a fresh suit and had shaved since their last encounter.

Bruce took a seat across the table from Thorn and returned the silent gaze before beginning. "Let's get right to this, shall we? You're here because you think I had something to do with the disappearance, correct?"

"You've done your homework." Thorn seemed surprised.

"It's my job," Bruce countered.

"Tell me, are you always this direct, or are you trying to impress me?"

Bruce didn't respond.

"Allow me to be equally direct. The thought did occur to me. I did some checking and it turns out that Meagan Bathurst is a client of yours."

"That's right. She retained my services eight months ago to help her find her biological parents."

"And that's why you're both in Sarnia?"

"Right again."

"Okay, so why would anyone want to grab here?"

"Beats the hell of me…" Bruce went on to tell him about Meagan's concerns that she was being followed by someone in a black limousine while they were still in Collingwood and his own personal opinion that she was just being paranoid. "… we were headed back to Collingwood when that idiot in the Dodge Dart drugged me and forced the car off the road."

"Did you get the plate?"

"No, the car was right up alongside of us before I realized there was a problem. After that I was in no condition to do much of anything."

"Well, that isn't going to be of much help to us. Would you recognize the occupants of the other vehicle if you saw them again?"

"I don't know, maybe. It all happened so fast, and I was more concerned with keeping the car between the ditches. I could try, though."

Thorn nodded slowly, still eyeing him as though looking for a crack in his story. "Would you mind looking through some mug shots?"

"No, not at all. In fact, if you're ready we can go right now."

"No need, I have them with me," Thorn said, reaching for a large briefcase.

"Do you normally make house calls?"

"No, not usually, but this is a crazy week down at the station. They're in the middle of a major renovation and we'd only be in the way."

Bruce's eyebrow peaked. "I see. Do you want to do it here or return to my room?"

"Here's fine." Thorn smiled.

The rest of the afternoon passed slowly as Bruce poured over the seemingly endless array of known felons. It was 4 pm when he finally closed the last of the books. The search had turned up nothing. Still the questioned remained: who would kidnap Meagan? It didn't make any sense. What could whoever they were possibly stand to gain from such an action?

The answer eluded him.

# CHAPTER 20

The sun was little more than a dimly lit patch of grey on the western horizon when a lonely barn finally came into view. Much of its exterior walls had long ago weathered away. AS they grew nearer, snow could be seen drifted heavily on the mounds of rotten hay.

Their bodies shivering uncontrollably, their feet painfully cold and sodden, they set a course toward the ancient structure. If nothing else, it might offer the possibility of being dry, and with the aid of Delse's lighter, it would be warm.

Conversation was held to a minimum. Their efforts concentrated on continued forward movement. Now, with a place of rest within reach, their limbs neared total exhaustion. The distance had been hard on all of them, but none more so than Meagan. Her previous injuries had slowed their efforts considerably. Many times she had asked to be left behind. The others refused to hear of anything so foolish. To leave her would mean her life.

A short while later they arrived at the barn and Meagan sat and rested while Delse and Julia set off in search of fuel. *Surely there has to be something around this old derelict capable of containing a fire*, Delse thought, poking through a pile of long-forgotten scrap. It didn't take long before she found exactly what she was after. An old, blackened forty-gallon drum lay on its side. A layer of ice formed since the last thaw held it firmly in place, but one solid kick from a frozen foot and the barrel rolled freely.

While Delse occupied herself with bringing the barrel into the barn, Julia made a discovery of her own—a roughed-in chicken coop. It was the size of a small bedroom, and the square opening leading to the loft above would serve adequately as a chimney.

"Delse, roll that in here," Julia instructed.

"Great. Meagan, come on, we'll be warm soon," Delse promised.

Meagan did not respond. The exertion and piercing cold had sent her into a numbing sleep—a sleep that could not be allowed to continue.

"Julia! Meagan's out! Help me!" Together they lifted her bird-like frame into the small room and placed her near the spot they intended to place the barrel. Meagan awoke once again, and Delse wrestled the barrel into place. Julia immediately began filling it with old papers and broken boards. The wood, dried over a millennium, caught quickly. Soon the small enclosure began to warm.

"Okay, I'm going upstairs to see about getting some straw in here," Julia announced. Delse turned her attention once again to Meagan.

After a while, once the room had warmed a little more and their toes had a chance to thaw, Julia, Meagan and Delse lay huddled together upon the mounds of straw Julia had retrieved from the loft. It smelled old and dusty, but none complained. Their thoughts were of the same thing; the one factor connecting them all together—the Forgiving Hearts Orphanage.

"I've been out there to see it," Meagan began. "It's just a burnt-out hulk now."

"Do either of you remember it?" Delse asked.

"No." This from Julia. "But then, I never had the slightest interest in finding my biological parents. The people who raised me are the only parents I need."

"Excuse me?" Meagan sat up. "You were never the least bit curious? Hell, that's why I'm down here in Sarnia in the first place. Delse, what about you?"

"What about me? I've always known I was adopted. Though it wasn't until I found a picture of my real parents after my adoptive father died that I began to understand. They looked very young." She grimaced. "Hell, I was likely the result of a leaky condom in the back seat of daddy's car."

"A little crude, don't you think?" Julie said.

"I should have called it a prophylactic?" Delse shot back. "Anyway, what's done is done. Finding them now after all these years is not going to change who I've become."

"I can't believe you two! Shit sakes! I even hired a private investigator to help find mine."

"What about the people who raised you? What about them?" Julia countered. "Don't their feelings mean anything to you?"

"Not knowing might be just fine for you, but it sure as hell isn't for me. I only found out that I was adopted a few years ago. Every waking moment since then I've wondered who I really am … where I came from. I don't feel it's unreasonable to want answers to those questions, and I really don't care if you agree with me or not. Two days ago, I didn't even know you existed."

"Hey, you two need to chill out!" Delse interrupted—she was becoming famous for it. "It isn't going to get us out of this mess any faster by you two clawing each other's eyes out. Mind you, a good cat fight would take my mind off of my frozen butt for a while," she mused.

All at once there was a stunned silence as Meagan and Julia sat staring, dumbfounded over Delse's candor. Of course, she was right, though her choice of words left nothing to the imagination. The tension, so high in the room only moments before, was gone as though it had never been.

"Look," Delse continued. "The three of us have always stuck together; we'll get through this too." A puzzled look fell across Delse's face the instant she finished speaking. "I don't know why I just said that."

"I feel it too," Meagan said.

"It's like I've known both of you forever," Julia added

"Shit's getting fucking weird up in here!" Delse proclaimed.

"Okay, so what do we do now?" Meagan asked.

"We should stay the night here and then at first light go in search of a phone," Julia said.

"Sure, and freeze to death...besides, what if the iron maiden decides to send her goons out looking for us?"

"Delse, we'll just have to deal with that when and if it happens," Julia said, sounding authoritative.

"No, Julia, Delse is right. You saw the size of those guys,"

"Yeah, I did, but remember— when they grabbed us all the first time, we weren't expecting it. If they try anything like that again we will be ready." There was a menacing tone to Julia's voice. It was one she had placed there intentionally, trying to ease the fears of her two companions. The truth of the matter was that she too was scared. She didn't like the idea of spending the night here anymore than they did, but common sense told her it was the best course of action. After all, traffic was bound to be almost non-existent on the roads now that the sun had set. Not only that, the image of their captors coming after them wasn't as far from her thoughts as she would have the others believe. It was going to be a long, cold night.

The night passed without incident and the next morning broke crisp and clear. Another light falling of snow adorned the ground. The roads, wet the day before, were now slicked with shimmering fingers of silver.

The barn far behind them now, the three walked on, cold and hungry, by the side of the road. Their lack of winter attire made the trek especially difficult. The cold was intense. Even those properly dressed would have been reluctant to venture forth as they had done.

"Meagan, do you believe in dreams?" Delse shivered

"Sure, I have them all of the time."

"No, I mean do you believe they could be warnings?"

"I guess anything is possible," Meagan replied. "You're still spooked, aren't you?"

"Of course I am, aren't you? I mean, this shit is too weird."

Julia walked ahead of them, trying to ignore their conversation.

"Sure I am, but right now I am more concerned with getting warm."

From a great distance, though growing nearer, a rumbling could be heard. Delse turned to investigate the source—a small speck on the horizon approaching from the rear. "Well, it's about freaking time!" she announced. What appeared to be a speck was actually a large eighteen-wheeler. "Ladies we are going to flag that sucker down."

"Are you sure that's a good idea?" Julia cautioned. "After all, we could be letting ourselves in for a whole lot of trouble."

"Personally, I would rather take my chances with a pervert trucker than stay out here any longer." They both knew Meagan was right. To allow the ride to pass would guarantee they froze to death long before they found a phone.

Though none uttered a word, the vote was unanimous. They turned to face the approaching truck, three shivering thumbs outstretched.

The driver's name was Michael Grey. He was a large man with light-brown hair, blazing hazel eyes and a well-muscled physique. At first sight, an imposing figure to be sure, however, upon closer inspection an entirely different impression would be gained of the man seated behind the wheel.

He was nearing exhaustion. Having driven through the night on the home stretch of his Montreal to Sarnia run, he almost didn't see the three half-frozen women on the side of the road. But as fate would have it, at the last moment he focused his road-weary eyes and brought the rig to a sliding stop thirty yards past the spot where they stood.

Still not trusting his eyes, he jumped down from the cab and quickly made his way to the back of the trailer for another look. Sure enough, three young women wearing only blouses and jeans were hurrying toward him. "Well, I'll be damned," he uttered, his disbelief still intact.

"Hey, big fellah, you got room in that rig for three frozen women in need of a ride?" Delse called out, having closed half the distance between them.

"How the hell did you three get all the way out here with no coats? Are you trying to freeze your asses off?"

"It's a long story. Can we get inside and warm up before we go into it?" Meagan urged.

"Yeah. sure, come on," he said, ushering them into the cab. "There is a thermos of soup and some sandwiches in the back if you're hungry. I picked them up a few hours ago, but you're welcome to it."

"Ah, thank Gawd. You're a prince," Delse gushed and wasted no time retrieving and dividing his offering.

"Here, wrap yourselves in these," he said as he reached back and produced two red and black checkered lumberjack blankets.

"Thank you. You can't know what this means to us," Julia said.

"I'm happy to help. I'm just glad I came along when I did. There's another storm front coming in from the Midwest. What's going on with you three, anyway?"

"You wouldn't believe it if we told you," Delse began.

"Try me?"

"Okay, but remember, you asked for it." She continued, "We were kidnapped, but we escaped yesterday and we have been trying to get back to town ever since."

"You're right, I don't believe it." He smirked, shaking his head.

"Maybe not, but it's the truth," Meagan said, picking up where Delse had left off. "This whacked-out old lady thinks that one of us is her heir given up for adoption as an infant. She had us followed and then abducted. She even tried to make us submit to tests that would determine whether or not she was right."

"Then what happened?"

"Meagan here pulled a knife on the old bat and we got away."

"Well, that's one name down, two to go. Mine is Mike."

"Oh, I'm sorry," Julia said. "My name is Julia and this is Delse. You already know Meagan."

"Well, it's nice to meet you girls, but what you're saying sounds too extreme to be true. I mean, the cops are going to have a tough time believing it, is all."

"Tell me about it," Delse agreed. "It did happen, though."

"Could you find this place again if you had to?" Mike asked.

"Bet your ass we could!" Again, Delse piped up, her cheeks brimming with ham and cheese on rye.

"Okay, so what can I do to help?"

"Getting us back to Sarnia is helping us enough. The rest we'll deal with ourselves," Meagan declared before Delse had a chance to speak again.

Julia said nothing. She sat staring out of the window looking for landmarks to help her find her way back here again. Meagan was right to decline further assistance from Mike, though they surely could use it. It just wouldn't be fair to get him involved, especially since they didn't even know him. For that matter, they really didn't know what they were involved in. Time would tell. She would feel much safer once they had a chance to talk to the police about all that had happened.

The truck crossed the outer limits of the city and soon afterward was coming to a stop in front of Julia's apartment building. Meagan and Julia thanked him for the ride and the food and climbed down from the cab. Delse lagged behind. Once she was sure the others were out of earshot, she turned to Mike and said, "The last name's Collier. If you feel up for a little adventure, I'm in the book. Call me." Then she too ducked out of the cab, leaving him with a puzzled look on his face.

"What did you say to him?" Meagan demanded.

"Nothing, I just thanked him again for all of his help."

"I don't know, Meg," Julia sighed. "Do you believe her?"

Meagan giggled, "Yeah…right."

There was a momentary exchange of laughter, a strange and sudden familiarity, as though they had known each other all of their lives. Each of them felt it, though none brought it to words.

Immediately upon arriving at Julia's apartment, nearly consumed with worry over Bruce's well-being, Meagan insisted on being the first to use the phone. She called the hotel she and Bruce were staying at on the off chance he might be there. He answered on the second ring.

Her relief at hearing his voice was complete. Her need to see him overwhelming. They had spent a great deal of time together over the course of this investigation and it had always been professional and on occasion confrontational, but it was difficult to rely upon someone as much as she had come to rely upon him and not come to care about them also.

Hanging up the phone, she turned to the others. "Bruce is on his way over here. He's bringing a cop with him."

"What have you got to drink around here?" Delse asked Julia.

"Liquor's in that cabinet," Julia said, motioning toward a credenza with frosted glass doors against the wall in the small dining area. "Help yourself."

Quickly locating the cache of booze, Delse selected a bottle of gin and a martini shaker. "Who wants?" she asked, holding the bottle and the shaker at shoulder height.

"Bring it," Meagan said.

Julia merely nodded, motioning "gimme" with one hand, eyes closed and rubbing the bridge of her nose with the other as though consoling a headache.

"Olives?"

"In the fridge," she said without looking up.

They were on their second drink when Bruce arrived, Constable Thorn in tow. Meagan stood as Bruce entered the apartment. The relief of his face undeniable, he immediately went to her. Taking her by the shoulders, he did a visual assessment of her before taking her into his arms and hugging her.

"Ahhh… easy!" she protested. "I got a bit banged up when we went off the road."

"I'm just happy to see you're alright. But I want to take you and get you checked out."

"Trust me, I'll live." She smirked.

"You are three very luckily ladies," Thorn chimed in.

"Who's Captain Obvious?" Delse asked.

"My name is Constable Thorn."

"Charmed, I'm sure," Delse said, bringing a hand to her forehead and rolling it toward him. The lack of sleep, food and the four shots of gin were beginning to take their toll.

Forty-five minutes later Thorn had taken each of them separately into Julia's bedroom and taken their statements. Delse was the last to emerge. Thorn told them he would have a plan-clothes cop posted outside of each of their homes and would be in touch. He left soon after.

No sooner had the door closed when Delse turned to the others.

"That fucker gives me the creeps."

Meagan looked tired and indicated to Bruce that she was ready to go back to the hotel. "Delse, if you're ready to go, we can drop you off at your apartment," Bruce offered.

"We can pick this up later, girls," Julia began. "I need a hot bath and a nap."

"I hear that," Delse agreed. "Ok Studly Do-right, lead on."

# PART TWO

It is by earth that we see earth, by water, water,
By air define air, and fire by destroying fire;
By love we perceive love, and hate by dreadful hate...

Unknown.

# CHAPTER 1

He had waited only an hour before looking up the number for Delse Collier.

He waited a day before making the call.

She had invited him over.

Now he stood outside of her door waiting for her to respond to the knock. He was nervous. This was new to him. Girls like Delse were new to him. Girls like Delse usually didn't like him. This didn't happen to him. What was he thinking?

The door opened.

She was as beautiful as he remembered. Her hair was spilling about her shoulders, and she wore only a white tube top and jeans, her nipples clearly visible, as though craving attention. There was a stirring deep within him. This couldn't be happening to him.

Who kissed who first was open to debate. In an instant, their lips met. The hunger was all consuming. A hunger returned. Nothing else mattered, only those lips, that touch, that body. Clothes melted away as though never there. Holding her against the wall, his thumbs caressed the curves of her breasts. There was no conversation. No expression of expectation. Fully engorged, he lifted her against the wall and plunged into her moist and welcoming body.

Now a crescendo of shrieks, breath and delight as he held her against the wall, nothing between them save the sudden unforeseen urgent need. Her hands seeking purchase on his chiseled back and shoulders. His powerful arms holding her against his muscled body, hard won from years of labour and only a passing glance at a gym, he plunged deeper into her, eliciting shrieks of pain, of pleasure.

Effortlessly, he carried her into the bedroom and, laying her down upon the bed, they melted into each other long into the night. When climax finally came, they lay in sweat-soaked sheets, giggling.

Sleep greeted them both soon after.

As dawn's first light revived them, their lips met yet again. The lovemaking softer this time, less urgent, gentler, but no less intense.

Kissing her deeply, his fingers gently caressed her cheeks as his body found hers and entered unopposed. He wanted to consume her. To be one with her. She was like no other woman he had ever known.

When it was finished, she watched him get up from the bed. He was beautiful. Michelangelo's David … if Michelangelo's David had a bigger dick. Leaning back over the bed, he kissed her.

"Hungry?"

"Starved!"

"Let me go see what you have in the fridge … see what I can do about that."

"You cook?"

"Yes, ma'am. My momma raised he right."

"She sure did," Delse said, stretching cat-like, the sheets losing their purchase on her breasts. "I think you should get back in here and cook before going in there and cooking." She smirked.

He rose to the occasion.

Having showered, Desle walked into the small kitchen to find Mike naked. His sculpted ass in front of the stove as he made whatever it was he was cooking. What had she been thinking? This guy wasn't like the other guys she was used to. She couldn't remember the last guy who had cooked breakfast for her. This one was good. He was what most would consider a "keeper." He was going to get hurt. She generally didn't do well with nice guys… *Fuck it,* she told herself. *Go along for the ride.* After all, so far it had been a pretty fun ride.

"What are you making? It smells wonderful."

"Slim picking in there," he said, indicting the fridge. "So I'm making us herb and Swiss cheese omelets."

"Well, it smells wonderful," she said, coming up behind him, her naked breasts pressing against his back she ran her hands around his slender hips.

"Careful now, you're going to start the launch sequence again," he said.

He turned off the stove and placed the pan on a back burner. He turned to face her. Breakfast was going to have to wait.

# CHAPTER 2

The name printed on the mailbox by the road was LEAP. Meagan mused that was exactly what she was doing … taking a leap. She knocked smartly upon the old wooden screen porch door and prepared her warmest smile. It was a long shot, but it was worth a try, especially since the conventional methods she had tried had come up short. She waited a few minutes before knocking again and was about to turn and leave when a gruff-sounding female voice stopped her.

"Whatever you're selling, I got six of them."

"I'm not selling anything, Mrs. Leap. I just want to talk to you."

"Well now, that's different." The old woman started toward the door but stopped short of reaching it. A veil of suspicion fell over her time-weathered face. "You aren't one of those 'Jo-Hoes,' are you?"

"No, ma'am."

"Well now, that's grand!" A wide toothless grin spread across her face. "Well, child, come on in, girl. You'll catch your death standing out there like a stick. Don't mind me a tick while I put my choppers in." Meagan did as she was told and followed the old lady through the kitchen into the den. "Don't get many folks around her anymore. Nope, not since that no-account son of mine…" She chuckled. "Well, will you listen to me. What can I do for you, sweetie?"

"I wanted to talk to you about the orphanage across the road," Meagan began. The old woman's face soured and the suspicion returned.

"Now, what concern is that old place of yours?"

"I spent five years of my life over there and I was hoping you could fill in a few of the blanks for me."

The suspicion left the old woman's face and in its place was the look of someone completely thunderstruck. "You were one of them?"

"Yes, ma'am. Do you know anything about what happened over there?"

Now the old woman, whose name was Norma Leap, looked uneasy to be in the same room as Meagan. "Keep talking, child, I'll put the kettle on." With that, she got up and moved into the kitchen.

Meagan fell silent and instead of talking to the woman through the wall she glanced around the room. It was probably typical for an old woman's home. The furniture was old, festooned with blankets and throw cushions, most of which likely dated back to the 70s. The room smelled musty, filled with fragments accumulated over a lifetime. A tiny fireplace with a shaved barn beam mantle adorned the wall opposite the door. On the mantle was an assortment of pictures housed in frames of various shapes and sizes. At one end was an old Kodak camera that looked ancient, and at the other was an equally old-looking pipe holder missing its pipe.

"Child, I could tell you stories that would give you nightmares for the rest of your days."

"Nightmares I got, what I want from you are some answers."

"But you were there … What good is an old woman's gossip to you?"

"Yes, ma'am. I was there, but for some reason I can't remember anything from that time in my life."

"Maybe its best left that way … not remembering, I mean."

"I have to know the truth about myself and what happened to me over there. If I don't, I swear I'm going to lose my mind."

"Good," Norma replied. "I just needed to be sure."

"Sure of what?"

"In the seven years that hell hole was owned by those Forgiving Hearts people a lot of evil visited itself upon the good folks living around here, to say nothing of the hell fire and blue-eyed torment endured by you poor youngsters staying across there."

"Evil … you must be exaggerating," Meagan said hopefully. Evil seemed like an extreme description, especially associated with an orphanage.

"Believe me, child, it was evil. But you can be your own judge." Norma darted a glance toward the window that looked out on the burnt-out hulk that had been the Forgiving Hearts Orphanage. "My family moved to this place in 1923. That place across there was built the year after by a Dutch immigrant. It was quite a big deal back then. Story goes that he had that place dismantled brick by brick in Holland, shipped to Canada and rebuilt here. Folks said it was an evil place right from the get go .... Hanged himself, you know."

"Who did?"

"Mister Dutch Immigrant himself."

"But why?"

"Found oil. Back then seemed everyone and his uncle was striking oil around here."

"He would have been a rich man …"

"He was already a rich man, but finding oil didn't make him any richer, not back then and not on that farm. People didn't know about mineral rights like they do today. Anyway, the town of Petrolia swooped in and claimed the rights and our Mister Dutch Immigrant went loco. Story goes that he poured cement on the hole and hanged himself on the third floor of that big old house." She pointed to the window and the house beyond without looking at it.

"That was foolish," Meagan began. "Couldn't the people of Petrolia just drill another hole?"

"Yes, you would think so, wouldn't you? The truth is, they tried… a dozen times, but never found the vein." She paused and gave Meagan a knowing look. "After that, the place saw no end to people coming and going. None of them stayed very long. Then in 1963 the Forgiving Hearts people bought the place…"

Meagan sat listening, waiting patiently for the old woman to say something that might be of some help.

"They stayed the longest … seven years. Probably would have stayed longer if it hadn't been for the fire in 1970."

"Did you ever speak to any of the people from over there?" Meagan asked, trying to give the woman's rambling monologue a direction to follow.

Norma paused for a moment, as though searching seemingly endless reams of memory before responding. "Nope," she said finally. "No need to, really, rumours were flying around here like a fart in a headwind." She giggled at her frail attempt at vulgarity.

Meagan smiled slightly. "Really, what were they saying?"

"Oh, all sorts of things … you know how some people can be. After a while half of what you hear is made up and the other half you can't believe."

"Surely there had to be some common thread to what they were saying?"

"There was, but it isn't right to talk poorly about the dead," she stated. Still, Meagan could see that it wouldn't take too much persuasion before she would tell all she knew.

"I don't want to know their names, only what they said. Surely that would be alright."

"I suppose you're right," Norma agreed. The kettle came to a boil and she left the room to tend to it. Moments later she was back with a tarnished tea set and put it on the coffee table.

"Well now, where was I?"

"You were about to tell me about the rumours."

Norma nodded. "Well, ever since that orphanage moved in over there, weird things started happening."

"What sort of things?"

"The livestock would go missing … not all of it, but some. That started right after they moved in." Her eyes narrowed. "Some said they were cutting it right there in the kitchen of that big old house. It was never proved, though."

"That's disgusting!"

"Imagine how the livestock felt." She grinned. "But that wasn't the worst of it. The children over there started dying."

"Dying!"

"Yup, hardly a month passed that the coroner didn't pay them a visit."

"That's awful! Did they ever find out why the kids were dying?"

"They had just started looking into it when the place burned, taking most of those poor little souls and most of the staff with it. After the fire, we didn't hear much about the goings on over there."

Horrifying images began flashing across Meagan's mind—images of screaming, desperate children trapped behind a wall of flames. Perhaps Mickey was one of those children, but that didn't seem to fit the dreams. No, she couldn't have been among the ill-fated kids on the third floor. After all, she had slept in the same room as her, Delse and Julia … wait … that wasn't right. It couldn't be. How could she possibly know which part of the house they had slept in unless she was beginning to remember?

Spurred on by the fuel of new knowledge and more questions, Meagan quickly thanked Norma for the tea and her time and left her sitting in the den.

Later that afternoon, Meagan brought her car to a stop in front of the Sarnia Public Library. The street was busy with a rush of holiday shoppers and so she had to wait a few minutes while a middle-aged man driving a beat-up Datsun cleared the parking space.

It was shaping up to be her lucky day. There were twenty minutes left on the parking meter, but just to be safe she deposited enough coins into the slot to bring it back up to a full two hours. Leaving the car, she started toward the double, tinted-glass doors of the library's main entrance. Inside the foyer, lighting seemed dim after coming in from the brilliant snow glare of mid-afternoon.

Three teenaged girls worked steadily behind the counter dealing with the ceaseless flow of out-going and in-coming books. Meagan took up a position at the end of the counter and waited to be acknowledged. The wait stretched into five minutes and normally this would have infuriated her, as she hated waiting, but the girls behind the counter were clearly doing their best to handle the traffic and were clearly short-handed. Meagan couldn't remember the last time she had been in a library with so much traffic. Finally, there was an ebb in the flow of knowledge seekers and one of the girls turned to acknowledge her.

"Hi, could you please tell me where I will find the microfilm section?"

"Certainly, ma'am," the girl chirped. This one didn't look older than fourteen. "It was moved over into the Lawrence house."

*Ma'am* – twenty-five years old and somehow she had become a ma'am. She shrugged it off. "The Lawrence house?"

"Yes, ma'am, its right across the street." The clerk pointed out through the doors at a large, seemingly out of place Victorian house on the opposite side of the street.

"Okay, thanks a lot." Meagan smiled and started toward the doors.

"You're welcome, ma'am," the young clerk called out.

Meagan cringed and pushed the door open.

The attendants in the Lawrence house were considerably older, and there Meagan was addressed as "Miss." She had to stop herself from saying "ma'am" when she approached the counter and asked for assistance.

A short time later Meagan found herself surrounded by reels of microfilm. The lady at the counter had been living in Sarnia during the time when the Forgiving Hearts controversy was in full swing and was very helpful when it came to dates and knowing which film contained what.

Meagan began her search with an article dated 16 July 1963. The story told of an orphanage recently set up out on the old Van Becke farm outside of Petrolia. The story made no mention of the origins of the property as told by Norma Leap. There were the usual public concerns regarding its presence in the area, but nothing that indicated any promise of a clash between the surrounding farmers and the proprietors of the orphanage. Then in May, a year later, the first of the deaths Norma had mentioned appeared in print. Hepatitis was listed as the cause of death and the orphanage had been placed under strict quarantine.

Two years later, in August, three girls were reported missing. A massive county-wide search for the missing children was conducted, but after two weeks of yielding no result the search was called off and the three were dismissed as runaways. Then, in the spring of 1969, a young family bought a recently parcelled plot of land and had begun building. It was then that the skeletal remains of three girls were discovered in a shallow grave. The coroner was quoted in the article and suspected foul play.

Meagan sat staring blankly at the screen. She felt as though someone had let all of the air out of her. "Maybe this has something to do with why none of us can remember," she murmured, and went in search of the next article. Apart from a rather extensive write-up a year later on the fire that consumed the orphanage and most of its occupants, there was nothing.

"We'll be closing in a few minutes, miss," the lady from the front counter said softly as she passed behind Meagan. "If you could please finish up whatever you are working on."

Meagan looked at her watch. The time had passed quickly. It was almost five-thirty. She made a hard copy of each of the articles she had found, and after neatly folding them in half she placed them in her purse. She had just finished closing the last roll of film when the attendant paused on route back to the counter. "I can put those away for you if you like, miss," she offered, reaching for the stack of blue plastic cases.

"Yes, thank you."

"Hopefully you were able to find what you were looking for." The woman smiled.

"Yes …. Yes, thank you, I did."

# CHAPTER 3

Susan looked worried as Julia strolled into the office after spending the morning with Tommy. In fact, they all did. There was a strange tone of accusation in their gazes and for reasons Julia could not explain, she felt guilty.

"Where the hell have you been all morning? I've been trying to reach you."

"Susan, what's going on? You knew I was with Tommy this morning."

Her lie exposed, Susan didn't have a chance to respond when Constable Thorn appeared in the doorway, drawing even more concerned looks from Julia's co-workers. Susan's back stiffened noticeably. "I told him you were out of the office and I didn't know when you would be back. He insisted on waiting in your office."

"Don't worry, I'll take it from here," Julia consoled, clearly unshaken with Thorn's presence. "Shall we go inside?" she suggested, raising her right hand and indicating a glass-enclosed conference room.

Thorn remained silent as he took a seat at the table. Julia followed and moved directly to the window. She stood with her back to him, surveying the winter-scape that only moments before she had been a part of.

"So, what's up?" Thorn asked.

"I want you to end your investigation into the kidnapping."

"Any particular reason I should do that?"

"Because I asked you to; there was no real harm done and I don't want my private life made public as a result of it."

"What about the other two? You speaking for them as well?"

"They'll agree to it once I explain my situation to them."

"Where are they, anyway? I haven't been able to reach them."

"I haven't seen them."

"What about the P.I. friend?"

"Couldn't tell you. He works for Meagan, not me."

"Why are you trying so hard to obstruct this investigation? What aren't you telling me?"

"I'm not trying to obstruct anything, least of all your investigation. While we're on the subject, if you had anything to go on you wouldn't be here badgering me."

"Are you nuts? You asked me here, remember? What are you afraid of, anyway?"

"I already answered that."

"I went out to that house, you know, the one with the gates and the dogs … there is nothing there. From the looks of the place, no one has lived there in a very long time, yet you and your friends tell me something entirely different. That tells me either the lot of you are lying to me or there is something larger than you realize going on here."

"Perhaps it's the former," Julia quipped, still facing the window.

"Sorry, I'm not buying it. Meagan's P.I. friend with the two first names believes it to be the latter and I tend to agree with him."

She turned to face Thorn. Hopefully he wouldn't notice the tears welling in her eyes. There was just too much to lose and clearly he wasn't about to break off his investigation. "You should leave now," she said, steeling herself against the sobs threatening just below the surface.

Not seeing any further progress being made, Thorn did as she asked and left the room without another word.

Julia moved to a nearby chair and collapsed into it. She closed her increasingly red and puffy eyes.

Susan, who had been standing in the doorway since Thorn's departure, finally asked, "Julia, what's going on?"

"Nothing that concerns you." Her voice sounded distant and defeated.

"Excuse me … I thought we were friends, and friends help each other, don't they?"

"Yes, you're right, they do. I just can't talk about it right now, okay?"

Susan didn't respond. She just stood there waiting for Julia to continue.

"Listen, Susan, I need to take a few days off. Could you have someone cover my cases?"

"You know the backlog we are facing here…"

"Please... just a few days."

"Well, I guess I could always have Helene cover for you. But you know that your cases won't get the attention they have been ..."

"I'm sure they'll survive."

"Yes, they will .... Will you?"

# CHAPTER 4

"You almost ready" Delse called as she went to answer the knock at the door of Meagan's hotel room. Opening the door, she found Julia, as expected, waiting on the other side.

"Julia's here— time to get that red mane under control."

"Yeah, yeah," Meagan sighed.

"You would not believe what it takes to get that chick bar-ready," Delse sighed. In that moment, Delse noticed that Julia wasn't exactly looking "club ready" herself. "Why am I suddenly getting the feeling that tonight is going to be a duo and not a trio of fabulous bitches?"

"Delse, I'm sorry, but I'm really freaked. I am so worried about my folks. I have to go see them and explain what's happened," Julia said.

Meagan emerged from the bathroom just as Julia finished speaking.

Delse turned to acknowledge her entry, "You get back in there or I'm coming at that mane with scissors." Then she turned back to Julia, "You see what I'm working with over here? Look… go take care of your shit. We'll be here when you get back."

"Thanks, Delse. Hey, Thorn was at my office today. He said he had his guys go out to that house. He said it was empty … said no one had lived there for years."

"Well, we know that's bullshit."

"I told him I wanted him to drop the case."

"Why'd you do that?" Delse asked. "Don't you want that old bitch caught?"

"Delse, I'm not like you. I wish I was, but I don't bounce back like you seem to. My folks are all I have and I need to protect them."

"Then go … protect them. We'll see you when you get back."

Outwardly, Delse was consoling. However, in her mind she plotted revenge… a means of neutralizing the threat that had become the common theme in each of their lives.

***

The space at the end of the bar was dominated by four large pool tables and around them were the usual assortment of blue-jean-clad hustlers and their marks. Over the tables set into the corner was a big-screen TV featuring a male bodybuilding completion. Meagan and Delse sat at the bar criticizing each contestant posing on the stage, marvelling at how such large men could fit into such tiny bathing suits.

"What a shame," Delse sighed.

"What is?" Meagan replied.

"Look at those poor guys … such beautiful bodies, but nothing below the waist worth going after."

"Yeah, I know. Give me a scrawny runt any day." Meagan giggled. All at once her eyes widened with delight. "Oh my God! Will you look at that?"

One of the guys playing pool, now aware of Meagan and Delse seated at the bar, was standing on the corner of the table imitating the men on the TV over his head. The show lasted only a minute or two before one rather frightening looking bouncer appeared and helped him back to the floor. Undaunted by the interruption to his performance, the young man turned and walked smartly to where the women were seated.

"How's it going, ladies?" he chimed.

"It's going great!" Meagan replied boisterously.

"Yeah, it's going great, so why don't you just keep on going." This was from Delse. Her tone was considerably less inviting than Meagan's.

The smile quickly faded from his face and moments later he was gone.

"That wasn't very nice," Meagan scolded.

"Ah, the guy was a loser."

"You don't know that. He might be a really great guy."

"No such thing."

"Oh? Not even that trucker friend of yours?"

"Who?"

"Come on, Delse, I know he called you," Meagan smiled. "I know you gave him your number after Julia and I got out of his truck that day."

"So what, guys are always calling me ... doesn't mean anything."

"Whatever," Meagan said, allowing the topic to drop momentarily. Obviously, this was not the best time to mention that she had invited him to join them. She'd just let it happen.

"You hear anything from that fancy constable of yours?"

"No, not yet. He should be back tomorrow or the day after at the latest."

"Do you miss him?"

"No, of course not!"

"Whatever."

"What the hell are you saying? The guy works for me, that's all."

"Bull."

"I can believe you just said that."

"Why? I've seen him. He's gorgeous."

"Yeah, well, we're strictly business."

"So, you don't mind if I take a shot at him?"

"Try it and kiss your kneecaps goodbye."

"Yeah, I thought so." Delse smirked.

There was a momentary silence between them. Meagan took a sip of her drink before speaking again. "I went out to the orphanage again the other day."

"What for? That place gives me the creeps!"

"Yeah, me too, but I didn't go to the orphanage itself. I went and spoke to an old woman named Norma Leap who lives across the road from the place."

Delse was intrigued.

"Yeah, I really had no idea what I was going to ask her, but as it turned out she was more than willing to do all of the talking."

"Did you learn anything?"

"Well, she said the place was evil..."

"Yeah, right! Come on, Meg, give me a break."

"I know, I know ... I thought the old gal was off her rocker as well, but Delse, when I left her place I went to the library and did some digging through the archives and guess what I found?" Delse only shrugged, declining the opportunity. "Four girls died there in the span of two years: One of hepatitis and the others were raped and strangled."

Meagan now had Delse's full attention. "So what are you getting at with this?"

"What if this Mickey we're all dreaming about was one of those four?"

"Could be, but there is also another possibility— what is she was number five…"

"Delse, take a look. He ring any bells for you?" Meagan's tone was low and threatening. A familiar face had suddenly appeared in the crowd. It was the old lady's driver. Meagan was first to pick him out.

"Ding dong … what's he doing here?"

"You really have to ask? Come on, let's make ourselves less visible. Maybe we can turn the tables on him."

"Good idea."

It wasn't a difficult thing to do. The bar was packed, and throngs of people pressed past the spot where they sat. One minute they were there and the next they were not.

They watched him closely from across the bar as they made their way along "Stud Alley" toward the exit. *Surely he wasn't still following us*, Meagan thought. He must know they would have gone to the police. Still, there he stood, tall and conspicuous amidst the hordes of college students.

"Do you think he saw us?" Delse asked, sounding more than a little concerned.

"Chances are he did. Let's not make it so easy for him this time, deal?"

"Deal."

Almost to the door now, Meagan glanced back quickly to get another fix on his location. He was gone. "Shit! I can't see him. Where'd that big bastard get to?"

The danger was behind them, not before. Walking backwards toward the door, they scanned the crowd. Still no sign.

Delse felt a large hand grip tightly around her arm. Fright forced a shriek from her lips. Adrenaline pounding in her ears, she wrenched her arm free, and with fists cocked she spun to confront her attacker.

"Delse, no!" Meagan cried. All at once Delse realized who it was that had grabbed her— Mike. There was an audible sigh of relief followed quickly by outrage. "You lousy son of a bitch! You scared the shit out of me!"

"You'll want to go home and change then," he joked.

"She'll have to scrape them out later. Mike, the old woman's driver is in here somewhere!" Meagan stated.

"Are you sure it's him?"

"Yeah, of course we are. Saw that fucker not three minutes ago, but then lost sight of him."

"Come on. Let's get you two out of here." With that, he began ploughing through the crowd, cutting a wide, easy path for them to follow. Moments later all three stood outside trying to get a handle on what was happening.

"Now you're certain he's here after the two of you?"

"No ... we're not," Meagan admitted. "I guess the sight of him just spooked us."

"Yeah, right! How many people do you know wear a freakin suit and tie to a bar!" Delse snapped. "He was looking for us. I am willing to put money on it."

"Okay, so where is he now?" Mike asked, looking around more for affect.

"How the hell should I know? The jerk was here."

While Mike and Delse went back and forth on the existence of the limo driver and his intentions, Meagan, having grown bored with the entire exchange, glanced soberly about the parking lot. At first glance, there appeared to be nothing of interest there either. She was about to rejoin the debate when out of the corner of her eye she caught the silhouette of a large vehicle parked by the side of the road some twenty yards from where they stood.

"Guys ..." she began.

"...Delse, all I said is I think you're being a little ..."

"Guys! Look!"

Instantly they fell silent as Meagan drew their attention to the large car pulling away from the curb.

"Any more questions? Come on, my car is right over there. I want to know where that ass hat is going." Without further conversation or dispute, Meagan and Mike fell in behind her. Moments later Delse's car, which had belonged to her father before his death, was bouncing out into the street.

Traffic was light and a layer of freshly fallen snow was making navigation considerably more difficult. If the driver of the other car knew he was being followed he was clearly unconcerned, as he continued to cruise along doing the speed limit.

"Have you thought about what we're going to do once that boat stops?" Meagan asked.

"Haven't gotten that far," came Delse's quick reply.

"Brilliant!" Mike quipped.

"For Christ sake, Mike, shut the hell up!" Meagan snarled. "If you want out we can stop right here!"

A smile touched Delse's lips. She had now met the tougher side of Meagan's nature for the second time since knowing her. She liked it.

"Just drive the fucking car, will you? And don't lose him."

"That's not in the plan."

The limousine finally slowed and turned into the underground parking garage of the Bayside Towers, a deluxe condominium high rise still only partially completed. It was billed as the elite as far as waterfront living was concerned, with only eight units on each floor. Most had been sold before the ground was even broken.

Delse pulled to the curb and got out to go the rest of the way on foot. She was clad in a short skirt and high heels—attire more suited for socializing that sleuthing—and the frigid night air, driven by the strong breeze blowing off the river, assaulted her legs mercilessly. Mike was the only one of the three properly attired for the weather and he was still bitterly cold.

"Come on, we need to get in there before that security gate closes," Delse instructed.

Their pace quickened and the staccato of heels impacted the icy sidewalk, echoing against the bordering buildings.

"How come you know so much about this building?" Mike asked, shivering.

"I play pool with a guy on the construction crew. He says that other than this gate there is no other security. It doesn't get activated for another month or so."

"Damn, but it's cold!" Meagan complained. "Delse, what happens once we get inside? I mean, where do we go?"

"That's simple. Most of the building isn't ready yet, just the model penthouse suite on the top floor. If there is someone staying here, that's where we'll find them."

"Makes sense," Mike agreed. "We'd better get a move on, that gate is not going to stay up forever." No sooner were the words spoken when the electronic whine from the gate's mechanism filled the night air.

"I can see it now, Delse. We're going to break our necks in these damned heels!" Meagan exclaimed as their pace increased past a precarious trot.

The date was closing too quickly. Mike knew he needed to act fast and ran ahead of the others, dropped to the ground and rolled under it. The laser tripped and the gate began to open again.

"I might just keep you around," Delse giggled as she and Meagan strolled into the garage.

"I just might let you," he groaned, getting to his feet.

They found themselves in a massive parking garage and though the building was not yet finished, a dozen cars dotted the parking stalls.

"I don't think we should take the elevator," Mike said, noticing a sign pointing the way to the stairs. "It would be too obvious. The stairs are over here, come on."

"Are you nuts? This building has sixteen floors and we're wearing heels," Delse protested.

"Take the damned things off," he said and started toward the stairwell. Both took his suggestion and soon were padding after him. The concrete slab floor was painfully cold against their nylon-clad feet, which only served to increase their pace.

To say the building wasn't yet complete was an understatement. Some of the floors consisted of only the outer shell of the building and naked beams reaching across the immense, gapping throat of the structure. The stairwell they found themselves in resembled just that—a well—only instead of descending into the earth, it rose into the sky amid the skeletal shell of the building. On the tenth-floor landing a door leading nowhere stood closed— closed for the simple fact that there was nothing but the cavernous innards of the building on the other side. In the fullness of time it would be sectioned off into individual units with floors and wall and windows and perhaps than it would look more inviting, but for now the sight bordered on the surreal.

"How much farther?" Meagan asked.

"Not too much ... maybe six floors," Mike replied.

"Wonderful!" This from Delse as she grasped the railing and started up yet another flight.

Suddenly the air was filled with sound. From somewhere above came the heavy footfalls of someone descending. Whoever it was obviously didn't expect to find anyone else in the building, because little care was taken to muffle the steps.

They were unable to remain where they were for the fear of being discovered. Mike motioned Delse and Meagan through a door leading to yet another unfinished floor.

This one was worse than the last one they had seen. Only steel girders spanned the crevice in a fifteen-foot grid pattern before giving way to a forty-foot drop—there was nothing to hang on to; only each other and the bare concrete wall.

Shoes still clenched firmly in hand, Meagan and Delse clung desperately to the wall next to Mike, holding their breath and listening as the stranger passed the door and continued his descent to the garage. Gingerly, Mike eased his hand around the door knob and gave it a twist. Opening it just a crack and peering through, he managed only to make out the top of the stranger's forehead as he went down the next flight of stairs.

"Damn." He had waited too long. "We may as well go all the way up and find out as much as we can while we're here," he offered and started through the door.

Meagan, following Mike's lead, started to inch toward the door as well. Delse, who stood farthest away on the girder, intent on not looking down, moved involuntarily in pursuit of Meagan. She was thrilled to be getting off of this ledge. Suddenly, hot agony seared through her left foot. Jerking it back, she saw the blood-covered tip of a two-inch metal sliver jagging menacingly from the edge of the beam. Already the beam felt slick with blood—her blood. Glancing down at her foot while trying not to see the forty-foot drop mere inches away, her stomach tightened. The tortured scream ready to erupt from her lips died in her throat. Below, the concrete floor loomed up, threatening to tear her from the ledge. Her knees felt watery and as her head began to swoon, the wall seemed to sway, frustrating her attempts to take hold.

"Meg…" Too late. Delse's feet lost their purchase on the ledge. Instinct took over. With arms flailing, her searching hands found Meagan's ankle, and they were now both were falling. Meagan reacted quickly and was able to turn her body inward to the wall. Her hands hit the ledge hard and clamped there, bringing the fall to a jerking halt. Four shoes plummeted into obscurity as Delse and Meagan, now dangling helplessly from Meagan's hold on the ledge inches from the blood-soaked sliver responsible for the current fix, concentrated their efforts on not falling any further.

"Holy shit! I'm slipping!" Delse screamed, madly groping for a better hold on Meagan's legs.

"Try and hang on! I'll get you up!" Mike instructed lamely. Neither of them had any intention of letting go.

"Hurry up! I'm slipping!" Delse screamed again now, clinging to Meagan's ankle.

"Please, Mike, hurry. I really don't want to die like this!" Meagan pleaded.

Bracing a foot on either side of the door jamb, he took hold of Meagan's upper arms and bore back hard. Meagan screamed in pain. The girder's edge was just too coarse to drag their combined weight over.

"Delse, it's no good. I'll hold Meagan, you try and climb up!"

"She's wearing nylons and a mini skirt, for Christ sake! What am I supposed to hang onto?"

"Okay, Meagan," he said, shifting his focus. "I'm going to let go of your right arm. I want you to reach down and help her out. Don't worry, I will still have a solid hold on you, so you aren't going to fall."

"Yeah, okay," Meagan gasped.

"Alright then, on three. One … two … *three!*

The switch was made smoothly and he now held her left arm in a mercilessly vice-like grip. It was going to bruise like crazy, but at this point she was beyond caring about bruises. Holding up to her end of the deal, she reached down and offered her hand to Delse. The other woman took it with a swift jerking movement. As she did, the weight shifted and another splinter ripped into the tender flesh of Meagan's underarm. She clinched her jaw against the pain. Moments later, a crimson perspiration stain soaked through and spread down the side of her silk blouse.

Below Meagan, Delse struggled, trying to get her flailing legs to cooperate. Each inch came and went slowly, painfully. Each upward move Delse made rocked Meagan's body, sending the already wounded arm harshly against the unforgiving metal.

"Delse! Move it!" Meagan screamed against the pain. "This girder is ripping my fucking arm off!"

"I'm trying!"

"You both have to stay calm!" Mike shouted to be heard over them. "Delse, you're doing great. You're almost home. Meagan, just hang in there a little bit longer."

Moments later, Delse's hand slapped the top side of the girder.

Now, without Delse's added weight, there was no problem pulling Meagan over the beam to safety, moments later to be followed by Delse.

The ordeal over, the three of them sat in the stairwell, their backs propped against the unpainted concrete, breathing a tortured sigh of relief.

"Mike," Delse began. "I think I speak for Meagan when I say you are not a fun date." There was no malice present in her voice and her eyes looked softer than he had ever seen them—almost inviting.

"Oh, I don't know, Delse," Meagan said, shifting her weight slightly and wincing from the pain radiating out from her armpit. "It wasn't all bad, but next time we should do something really fun …"

"Yeah, like getting our wisdom teeth pulled!" He laughed. "Come on, let's get out of here."

"What about the penthouse?" Meagan asked, the blood flow from her wound increasing.

"Forget about it for now. We know that it's here and right now we need to get you both to a doctor before you bleed to death."

There was no argument from either of them, and with that they rose to their feet and started down the first of sixteen flights that awaited them.

By 2:30 am they were leaving the emergency ward of St Joseph's hospital. Their story of having had too much to drink and getting too close to the edge of the walkway framing Sarnia Harbour seemed to be effective enough in raising no further suspicion. Stitched, bandaged and sore, Meagan was dropped off by Mike at her hotel before he drove to Delse's place.

# CHAPTER 5

The last wisps of silver chimney smoke faded into the cloud-covered night sky. Outside, blue, red and green spotlights illuminated the front of the house, while inside the windows were charged with dream-filled darkness.

Her first visit in six months. Perhaps she should have called first. The place looked as it did when she left, but somehow it was all so very different. At least it would be once she went inside. Not yet. She didn't want to face that yet.

Sliding down in her seat, leaning her head against the rest, Julia gazed soulfully out through the windshield. The steady beam of the headlights exposed a small stand of snow-laden spruce bordering the property. A lone raccoon moved momentarily into the scope of the light before waddling back to safer harbours beneath the branches of the tallest of the trees.

Parents. They weren't hers, not really. Still, she loved them. How would they react when she told them? She knew only too well. She dreaded that reaction. They were bound to be hurt by this; there was no question. They wouldn't say much, but their eyes would say all they couldn't bring to words.

The raccoon was back. His eyes glowed fiery green. Julia watched him a moment longer then killed the lights, allowing his nightly perusal to continue undisturbed. She shut off the engine and got out of the car. Standing next to it gazing up at the house, memories began to flash through her mind— some happy, some not so. The new car wrecked while she was learning to drive at sixteen. The puppy for Christmas the first year she was adopted. The laughter. Oh, how they had laughed when that lope-eared pup jumped for a dishcloth draped off the edge of the counter and ended up wearing that evening's Caesar salad. A smile graced her lips as memories of that silly little hound returned to her. As quickly as the smile appeared it was gone. Another memory now controlled her awareness. This one different from the others. Distant and fragmented, and somehow, dark. Liquid chills raced the length of her spine while thoughts of that other time, that other place, danced elusively before her eyes.

The memories were always the same. Always fading before she could figure out what she was remembering. The child psychologist she had visited following her adoption said it was a mental block her mind had constructed to protect her from something that had happened when she was still very young. Other than that, the shrink was of little help explaining or helping to uncover it. Each session had only left her with more unanswered questions— questions with their elusive answers that in dreams would swim dangerously close to the surface of that murk, leaving her nights sweat-soaked and sleepless to this day.

Shaking free of the past for a while longer, she started toward the house. Freshly fallen snow lay inches deep and wet on the front walk. Come morning, the man she called Dad would emerge, shovel in hand, to clear it away, only to repeat the task following the next onslaught.

Her stomach did a slow forward roll as she rang the doorbell. It dingdonged merrily within. Why hadn't she just used her key? she wondered silently. Perhaps now, in light of all that had happened, in light of what she had come to say, it would have been taking too great a liberty.

Julia was seven years old again, standing at the door holding the hand of the social worker. The door looked huge, imposing. She was terrified of what could possibly lay beyond. The social worker tried tirelessly to ease her doubts and fears, and still Julia couldn't help but feel empty, unwanted … alone.

Minutes passed before one by one the lights were turned on inside the house. This had always been his way when answering the door in the middle of the night. He always started with the switch at the head of the stairs followed by the hall light located just inside the door and then finally the brass coach light over the mailbox. The sound of the deadbolt recessing filled the frosty night air and the door swung open. There was a puzzled look on his face when he realized it was her. He quickly shook it off and ushered her inside.

"Why didn't you call and let us know you were coming?" he asked, more out of concern than inconvenience.

"It was kind of a spur-of-the-moment thing."

"Yes, well you're here now. Take your coat off. Let's get you warmed up."

"Sounds good to me," she began. Somehow the words sounded wrong. She had come here to rob them of something they had cherished for many years and was helpless to feel anything but undeserving of his love, his kindness. "Dad, I'm sorry for waking you…"

He waved her apology aside, not allowing her to finish. "I was just about to come down for a snack, anyway." It was an obvious lie; one she had heard him use far too many times while growing up to not recognize it now. She loved him for it. "Come on, let's go make us one of those triple-decker salami, onion and peanut butter sandwiches your mother's always saying I shouldn't eat."

"Shhhh!" Julia brought her finger to her lips in conspiracy. She didn't have the heart to tell him that mother had long ago filled her in about the so-called restricted culinary monstrosity. Through the years of making their infamous sandwiches, neither of them had ever actually eaten one. Mother's timing was always perfect to save them from the acute gastral distress that would surely ensue following the consumption of such a combination.

"Hi, sweetheart" Julie's mother Marie shuffled into the kitchen wearing fuzzy slippers resembling beer cans.

"Hi, Mom. Nice slippers!" She giggled. "Lose a bet?"

"Your father's idea of a joke." She smirked.

"What, you don't like them?" he protested, trying to sound hurt through his grin.

"Did you drive all the way here through that storm!" Marie demanded, standing next to the window.

"I had to see the two of you," Julia began without meeting their eyes. "Something has come up and I don't want either of you to be hurt by it, but I fear it's unavoidable at this point."

"Sounds serious," he said, pushing the ingredients for the sandwich aside as he had done countless times in the past.

"It is."

"Okay, so don't keep us waiting. Sweetheart, what is it?"

"A few days ago, I was kidnapped along with two other women…" Marie eyes widened in terror as an audible gasp escaped her lips. "…As you can see, I'm fine. We all are. We managed to get away and the police are investigating."

"I don't understand," her dad began. "Why would anyone want to kidnap you, and now that you're safe how could that hurt us?"

"Well, the woman behind the abduction claimed that one of us is her heir, who was given up for adoption…"

"I see," Marie sighed, exchanging a concerned glance with her husband. "And how did she expect to prove that claim?"

"She demanded that each of us submit to several tests, but we refused and shortly thereafter we managed to get away."

"And the police say what?" he probed.

"The man in charge of the investigation doesn't know what to think. He's sent men out to that house where we were being held and found nothing. He said that the house appeared not to have been lived in for a very long time," Julia explained. "But that can't be, because just the day before there were people living here. Hell, the place was furnished like a museum."

"Obviously this mystery woman doesn't want to be found," Marie observed.

"Yes, and is going to great lengths to avoid it."

She went on to tell them of Meagan and Delse and their involvement in the ordeal. And how other than the Forgiving Hearts Orphanage there didn't seem to be anything the three had in common. She told them how all of them had been followed for weeks by someone driving a limousine before the kidnapping.

"Do you think these people are still following you girls?" her father asked, his concern unstopped and flowing freely in his voice.

"I can't be sure. This whole thing has me so jumpy, I'm starting to think the whole world is out to get me."

Marie got up and left the room, returning a short time later with a collapsible file folder. There was a strange sadness spreading across her father's face as her mother spoke. "We should have shown this to you long before now, but I guess we were afraid to, especially with all those terrible nightmares you had growing up." There no protests from her father as Marie removed the elastic holding the file intact and pulled its contents into the light for the first time in a very long time.

"Mom, what's all that stuff?"

"This is your history."

"My what?" Julia gasped. It wasn't supposed to be this easy.

"As your mother said, we should have shown this all to you long ago, but it seems you need to know now more than ever."

"First," Marie began. "This woman claiming to be your biological mother isn't. Your birth mother, from what I could find out in my research, died in childbirth. There was never any mention of who your father might have been."

"What was her name?"

"Donna Webster. It says here that she was eighteen when she gave birth."

"And when she died," Julia added.

"Evidently. There is also a note written in that you were to be taken directly to that horrible place immediately following your birth."

"Weren't there any relatives that could have taken me in?" Julia was appalled. It sounded wrong, ungrateful, but to try and recant it now would only complicate matters further.

"I don't know the answer to that one, sweetheart," Marie continued. "The space for the next of kin was left empty on her records."

"So, it's possible that the woman who had us kidnapped could be some kind of relative."

"It's possible. What are you going to do?"

There were those eyes, eyes filled with sorrow Julia had known would soon appear. Clearly, while Marie was the one to research and ultimately the one to disclose Julia's past, she had stacked hope upon hope that she wouldn't want to take it any further. Funny thing about hope—it was seldom reasonable.

"At this point, I really don't know." She sighed. The truth was, she did know. Finding out the truth, at least this much of it, only succeeded in bringing more unanswered questions bubbling up to the surface. She didn't want to hurt these wonderful people, but not knowing the rest of the story would end up driving her completely crazy. She could only hope they would understand.

# CHAPTER 6

Her foot heavily bandaged and throbbing, Delse made her way through the crowded halls of Sarnia Secondary toward the library, drawing dull curiosity from those she passed that noticed her at all. It had been eight years since she was here last. She remembered how glad she had been to put this place behind her. She hated it, hated almost everything about it, believing there was nothing to be learned here that would ultimately help her in her day-to-day life— apart from some street smarts, she had been right. Yet here she was, returning in search of answers— answers to questions she had only recently learned how to ask.

Leaving the halls, she passed through the sensor-monitored entrance of the library and immediately scanned the room for the attendant. Classes were about to begin, so with the exception of those students with first period study hall, the carpeted vault was mostly empty.

She quickly located a matronly-looking woman ,who had to be pushing sixty, menacingly brandishing a metre stick like a drill sergeant as she strolled sour-faced through her domain.

"Hello, Mrs. Church," Delse said, walking up to her. "You probably won't remember me. My name is Delse Collier. I was a student here eight years ago."

"A student, dear?" she replied. "Is that what you call what you were?"

"So you do remember."

"Yes, dear, I remember." Her tone was much softer. She prided herself with not forgetting a single student ever to pass through those double glass doors. "I didn't expect to see you back here, though. What brings you back to us?"

Delse produced the photographs she had taken from her father's house and handed them to her. "I'm trying to learn the identity of the girl in this picture."

"Nice-looking girl. 1965, ah?" she said, turning the picture over and reading the date printed on the back. "A bit before even my time here. Who is she to you?"

"She might be my mother," Delse replied.

"Your mother!" Mrs. Church looked up astounded, locking Delse's eyes.

"Yes, I thought maybe old yearbooks…"

"That is definitely one option, but why not start with the orphanage itself? Surely they would be able to assist you more fully."

"I thought of that as well, but I came from the Forgiving Hearts Orphanage and it burned down with all of its records years ago," Delse explained.

"Yes, I can see how that would make it a little difficult. Well, come on. Let's go see what we can dig up." She smiled. "Just give me and minute and I will be right with you." With that, the infamous Mrs. Church strode over to the reception desk to retrieve a set of keys and to leave instructions with her student assistant.

She returned moments later, "Okay, let's go."

She led Delse through the library stockroom to a padlocked white metal door. It was the library's cold storage vault where temperature-sensitive historical documents were stored. Delse found herself wondering what possible need a high school library could have for such an elaborate preservation method as this. After all, they were only yearbooks; pages upon pages of ill-considered haircuts, questionable style choices and unrealized dreams quoted in perfect penmanship stretching back through the years. Surely they weren't worth anything, yet here they were locked away with the other so-called important documents.

As the door opened they were greeted by a brief cloud of mist and the ever-present odour of old books. "Why keep it so cold in here?" Delse asked.

"Helps keep the mold down and the worms from eating the paper," she explained, scanning the shelves for the yearbook dated 1965. Finding it in seconds, she turned and ushered Delse back into the warmth of the stock room and closed the vault door. "Okay, now, let's see. From the looks of the girl in this picture, I'd say she was roughly seventeen and that would put her in the eleventh grade." She was thinking aloud, flipping through the pages to the class rolls.

Delse stood next to her scanning the pages as well. However, it was Mrs. Church who finally plucked the face from the page. "Ah hah! There you are … Cindy White," she announced triumphantly. "Mind you, this was taken many years ago, and is she bound to have been married. The name will be different now."

"That's okay. At least now I have a name to go on now. That's more than I had when I got here. Thank you."

"Glad I could help."

"And you have, greatly. Again, thank you for all your help." At that, Delse turned and left her old nemesis/newfound friend. Stepping into the now-empty corridor, she took her a renewed sense of purpose, of hope in a quest that had never been hers but was now. With that purpose, the hope, there was an eerie feeling. Four years she had walked these halls. How strange it felt, now that her search had begun, to realize that the person she sought had once walked these very halls, and whose identity had always been just beyond those doors leading into the library.

From an adjoining passage, a well-bearded man smelling of Old Sail tobacco, an unlit old pipe clinched in his teeth, appeared and hurried past. Delse breathed deeply, smiling at the pleasant aroma. Suddenly, something odd began to happen. The walls loomed in toward her and somehow changed.

**"DANNY, NO! I DON'T LIKE THIS GAME!"**

"Miss Collier…" Mrs. Church called. "Oh, I'm so glad I caught you."

"Mrs. Church, is something wrong?" Delse asked, still feeling slightly dazed by what had just happened.

"You forgot you purse, dear." She smiled.

"Oh, right, thanks." Delse didn't remember having set it down. Accepting the bag, she shivered weakly and hurried from the building by way of the main lobby.

Thirty minutes later she sat across from Mike in a little pub off of Christina Street, their drinks and food order taken.

"What did you learn at school today, dear?" he asked, as though he was speaking to someone who was actually still in school.

"Ha ha, very funny," Delse replied. "Just a name." She pulled the picture of the young couple from her bag and put it on the table. "That is Cindy White," she said, pointing to the girl in the picture. "My mother."

"That's great! Do you know where she is now?"

Delse shook her head. "That was a long time ago. She probably got married, might even be dead. In any case, her name is probably different now, so it's not like I can just look her up in the phonebook."

Their food and drinks arrived and Delse put the precious picture back in her bag for safekeeping. The conversation dwindled as they ate their lunch, but an idea began taking shape in the back of Mike's mind.

"Did you get a hold of Julia?" he asked.

"I left a message on her machine to meet us at my place."

"Okay, good." He was no longer interested in his food. "Hey listen, I have something I want to look into before we get everyone together. After we're done here I'm going to drop you off at your place."

"What is it?

"Just a hunch. I don't want to say anything in case it doesn't pan out."

"Someone's being mysterious."

"Just trust me. I shouldn't too long."


The eleven o'clock sun shone down brightly upon the previous night's blanket of snow, bringing to life millions of tiny mirrors that lay hidden amidst its icy façade. Row upon row they stood, silent sentinels of life now gone, and for some, forgotten.

The air was strangely still, the cold intense, as Julia made her way toward a large marble angel. The attendant said she would find the grave in this area of the cemetery, but had not offered to show her the way. She couldn't blame him, really. After all, it would not have been her first choice for a cheerful winter's morning either.

There was something strange about a cemetery during the winter. Perhaps it was simply the finality of winter's seemingly endless ice-lock wrapped around the stones bringing the realization of death to the fore. Maybe it was just cold.

Since leaving her parent's house earlier that morning she had thought of nothing else. She had to come and see for herself before it would be real.

The look on her parents' faces as she was leaving, both knowing what her next move would be, weighed upon her like a lead backpack. She hated the way this had hurt them, how it had silently changed all of their lives, but with the pain already there and the sores now flowing freely she might as well satisfy her need to know.

She pushed the thought of them from her mind and trudged forward toward the final resting place of a woman she had never met. The same woman who, by all accounts, had given her live to give life to her.

"Stop it! Don't romanticize this," she scolded herself aloud. "Don't put this situation into one of you pretty little boxes."

She was now standing over the humble stone of Donna Webster. "They tell me that you are my real mother," she began. The inscription on the stone read: **Survived by her loving brother Richard and one sister Brenda.** "I've thought a lot about you and who were … why you gave me away." A tear fell from the corner of Julia's right as she realized the loss she might have known if the circumstances had been different. "The people who raised me are really nice and they love me …" The words stopped coming. What was there to be said? "Good bye, Momma."

With that, Julia lay a single red rose atop the stone, turned and walked away.

A slight breeze stirred from the north, caressing the snow from the branches of a nearby tree, and for the briefest of moments Julia felt sure she saw someone out of the corner of her eye. Without looking again, she quickly resigned herself to the impossibility of it, and continued toward her car parked near the entrance.

Had she turned to see if indeed there was someone there, perhaps she would have seen the shadowy image of a little girl against an endless sea of white and stone.

The others were waiting for her. For reasons she didn't understand, a meeting had been called for 1:00 pm at Delse's apartment, and she was already late. Possibly some development in the case, but whatever it was about, she really wasn't interested. Too much was changing, and more than ever there were far too many loose ends refusing to fit into the tightly wrapped box she called life.

Turning onto the street where Delse lived, Julia was surprised to see that it was only two streets over from where Tommy and his mother lived—not her favourite side of town, to say the least. Yet one she was well acquainted with.

Upon arriving at the door to Delse's apartment, conversation could be heard filtering into the hall from within. There were male voices present and from this Julia deduced that Mike and Bruce had been included in the gathering. Knocking twice, Julia opened the door and found Meagan, Delse, Mike and Bruce all huddled around a small, humble coffee table.

"Well, it's about time. Where have you been?" Meagan chirped, noticing Julia as she entered.

"The cemetery," came the curt reply, which brought puzzled expressions to the faces of both men present.

Aware of their bewilderment, Delse provided the solution they sought. "Julia found her mother."

Almost simultaneously, their bewildered expressions changed to grimaces as they realized what was implied, and they said nothing.

"So ... what's so urgent that you called this little meeting?" Julia asked, her tone bordering upon condescending.

"The old lady's back," Delse offered.

"Yes, so?"

"So, after you left last night Delse and I were followed to the depot by the old lady's driver," Meagan began. "Mike showed up and we were able to turn things around. He led us to the Bayside Towers ..."

"Aren't those still under construction?"

"Let me finish. The model suite is already completed. And we assume that that's where the old lady is now operating out of."

"You assume ... so, you're saying that none of you actually checked it out?" Julia scoffed.

"We ran into a little trouble on the way up and had to turn back," Mike stated, becoming more than a little annoyed by Julia's suddenly negative attitude.

"Sounds like you're batting a thousand."

Bruce, who had remained silent up until now, jumped into the conversation. "Julia, we're only telling you this because you are involved and we felt it only right that you should be aware that the danger is still not over."

"Yes, well... I suppose gratitude is in order, but you see, I'm not involved any longer. I have found out who my biological mother is, or was, and now I intend to get on with my life. These other two have the mystery. Please don't try to drag me into it any longer." With that, Julia turned, leaving the apartment and the others staring dumbfounded at the spot from where she had given her speech.

Meagan held the gaze longest. The change in Julia was so sudden and such a complete contrast from the person she and Delse had come to know. More and more it was becoming clear to her that Julia wanted no part of any possible friendship. It saddened her, for what could be so terrible—what had happened to change her so?

"Okay, back to business," Bruce said. "Meagan, your folks are still not willing to budge where giving us access to your adoption paperwork is concerned. And that just leaves us with this mysterious old lady as our only lead."

"Wonderful." She sighed. "If that's the case, I doubt I really want to know after all."

"Meagan, you don't really feel that way, do you?" Delse asked. "I mean, come on, you've gotten this far, don't turn back now."

Meagan smiled, but offered no other response.

"That brings us to Delse's good news," Mike piped up. Instantly, her face was alight, for he had been fiendish in the way he had refused to divulge the information. "Now, I'm no private investigator, but I was able to track down the name you gave me through the registry office here in town and from that I came up with a phone number and an address."

"But how? I only told you the name this morning ... I had no idea it would be..."

"Now, the address is two years old," he stated, intentionally cutting her off. "But it's a place to start..."

"Mike! For Christ's sake, tell her before she explodes!" Meagan snapped.

Smiling from ear to ear, he began again. "12785 Waterworks Side Road. Her last name is different, though. She married a guy by the name of Metcalf." He paused momentarily, studying her face. Then all at once a cross expression came upon him. "Well, what are you waiting for? She's expecting you at three-thirty!"

"What!" Delse gasped. "You've already spoken to her!" He tossed her a coy wink followed by a slow nod. "Mike, I could kill you for this!"

"What did I do?"

"It's one-fifteen now. What am I going to say to her? "

"What are you going to wear?" Meagan offered this factor to puzzle.

"My God, I never even thought about that!" Delse was nearing a complete nervous breakdown by this point. "Meagan. You've got to help me!"

"Don't worry, I will." Meagan assured her. "But first there is something else that needs to be taken care of …"

"Oh, what?"

"Mike? Bruce?"

"Yes."

"Get out. We ladies have a lot of work ahead of us and we don't need the two of you issuing half-time reports."

"Yeah, yeah. I'd rather play pool anyway. Come on, Bruce, I know a place not far from here."

Moments later, Delse and Meagan were left standing and staring at each other. The gaze lasted only a few seconds, though it seemed longer, then, with no words passing between them, the starter's pistol exploded and the race was on.

# CHAPTER 7

Julia's car sat idling in the street in front of the townhouse Tommy and his mother shared. She didn't have an appointment and by rights shouldn't be there, but she had been close by and so decided to stop in unexpectedly.

Minutes ticked past like hours while she sat staring at the sad and run-down dwelling.

The front window, clothed by only a torn bed sheet, the pale blue paint on the front door badly cracked and peeled, exposing the pressed-board door below. In the drive, up on blocks, were the remains of a rusted green sedan. It hadn't seen the road in many years and just being there violated the housing by-law, but that wasn't her concern. She knew what she was about to encounter. A screaming drunk presided over the pigsty that lay beyond that door. She also knew that if she were to go in there she would have no choice but to remove Tommy from the home.

With Christmas a little over a week away, she wrestled with the thought of actually going through with it. Not to mention Susan's constant warnings to avoid it at all cost. Perhaps the situation would keep until after the holidays. Reaching for the steering column, she shifted the car into drive and moved out into the flow of traffic.

# CHAPTER 8

The sky was a deep blue/grey and growing darker to the northwest, threatening yet another storm when Delse eased the car to a stop on the ice-slicked road. Ten yards away was the entrance to Mrs. Metcalf's driveway, bordered on both sides by an eight-foot coral-coloured brick wall. Snow drifted heavily against it, yet evidence of a hedge row running in front of it could still be seen. Above the hedge in large brass script, 12785 WATERWORKS was embossed on both sides of the opening. There was no gate denying entrance; only two large brass couch lamps glowing warmly through the afternoon gloom.

Three-thirty had come too early. And as Delse sat studying the wall and its brass-work, she felt sure she wasn't ready for what was about to come. She wasn't even sure why she was there in the first place. Or what she hoped to gain from it. Julia had said it many times—this was Meagan's dream, not theirs. Still, with realizing the object of her own unintended quest so close at hand, guilty feelings began to flicker somewhere near the back of Delse's mind. It had come about too easily for her while Meagan met with resistance after resistance in the search for her birth parents. Meagan had done nothing to instill the guilt; in fact, she had only been too happy for her, but the pain was there.

She glanced into the rear-view mirror to make sure Meagan's make-up job was still covering the dark circles under her eyes. How many nights had it been since she managed to sleep without dreaming of the little girl? She did not know, but at least the dreams were becoming more pleasant. Somehow, the little girl had became more and more excited as Delse did. No, they were no longer nightmares, yet they still woke her sharply, robbing her of rest. She had asked Meagan if she was still having the dreams that very afternoon, and she said that she was also, but they weren't as frightening as they had once been. Neither of them dared to ask Julia. She had made it quite clear that she was completely unapproachable on the topic.

Delse removed her foot from the brake and allowed the car to roll forward into the mouth of the drive, and now all that lay hidden behind the coral wall was revealed. A long, key-shaped drive of red paving stone, completely cleared of snow and bordered by perfectly shaped pines, glistening with tiny clear Christmas lights, brightened the way to the house approximately maybe fifteen yards distant from the road. One lane branched off the main and disappeared around the right-hand side of the house and Delse assumed they led to outbuildings located beyond her field of view. The house itself, constructed of the same coral brick as the wall, was an immense bungalow. It arched forward, emulating the shape of the drive, and large windows told of the warmth within.

Removing the key from the ignition, Delse got out of the car and stood momentarily in awe of this rural paradise, finding it harder still to believe this woman could be her mother.

The aroma of something sweet baking drifted out through the heavy twin teak doors. The urge to run was strong. Surely this woman was not about to accept her.

*Why put yourself through this*, she thought.

Finally, curiosity took a stronger hold and Delse reached up and pressed the doorbell. Instantly the air filled with the melody of Westminster chimes and moments later the door was opened.

"Yes, what may I do for you?" asked a young man in his late teens.

"Is Mrs. Metcalf in?"

"Who is it, Peter?" came the voice of a woman, accompanied by hurried footsteps on hardwood.

"Don't know. Haven't asked her yet."

All at once, Peter was pulled from the picture and the door opened wider, exposing Mrs. Metcalf. "You'll have to excuse my son—over protective and all that, you understand."

Delse smiled and nodded that she did indeed understand.

"You must be Delse Collier?" she said, ushering her in out of the cold and closing the door behind her.

"Yes, ma' am, I am."

There was a moment of silence, a moment that went on for hours as each of the women stared at the other in curious wonderment. Finally, Mrs. Metcalf broke it.

"Please, let me take your coat. We can talk in here," she said, showing Delse to the den off the front hall. "I must tell you your gentlemen friend took me quite by surprise and…"

"Perhaps I shouldn't have come," Delse said, hesitating.

"No, no, not at all. I'm glad you did. Come in, sit down. You have no idea the number of sleepless nights I've spent wondering what became of my daughter."

Over the mantle was a large oil painting of a woman, and when Delse saw it her eyes widened and her back went stiff. "You're assuming that I am indeed that daughter. What makes you so sure?"

"I look at that picture at least three times a day. You bear a striking resemblance to her.

How could I have any doubts?" Mrs. Metcalf announced joyfully.

"Who is she?"

"My mother. She died three years ago, rest her soul. She never forgave me for giving you up."

"Why did you?" Delse asked softly, not really sure she wanted to know the answer.

Mrs. Metcalf anxiously bit at her lower lip. The question was one she had to be expecting, yet it seemed to shake her terribly. Taking a long deep breath, she met Delse's eyes and began.

"It was very different then. You have to understand. I was only sixteen when you were born, still only partway through school and with no way of supporting myself, let alone a child to boot."

"What about your mother? She couldn't have helped you?" Delse pressed.

Mrs. Metcalf cast her eyes to the carpet and shook her head. "My mother was a very religious Pentecostal woman and didn't understand how a daughter of hers could commit such a dreadful sin. She made me give you up."

"But you said she never forgave you?"

"That's right, she didn't. Mothers are a very bizarre breed." Tears were welling in her eyes as she spoke. "She deprived me of the life I might have had with you only to make my life with her a living hell."

"Why didn't you ever try to find me? Not even after she died?" Delse added.

"I tried. Lord knows how I tried, but I had nothing to go on. I didn't even know if you were still alive, and when I found out all the records were destroyed in that damned fire …Delse … can you ever forgive me for what I did to you?" she pleaded.

"You gave birth to me. You need no forgiveness for that. As far as the rest of it, well, it wasn't your fault."

"I doubt I could be so understanding were the situation reversed."

Delse smiled weakly and lowered her eyes.

"Was it terrible for you …growing up?"

"Difficult. There wasn't much love in that family. He was a drunk and he blamed me for their marital problems caused by his drinking. She, well, she enjoyed the company of other men. I doubt he even wanted to adopt a child…no, scratch that, I'm certain of it. He told me enough times. Anyway, they split up halfway through my teens. I left home shortly after that.

I've been on my own ever since."

"Did he harm you?" Mrs. Metcalf asked. Strangely, a maternal strength rose within her.

"No, not the way you mean. Not the way that breaks the skin or raises bruises. He died a short while ago and there are times when I definitely hate him. And then again there are times when I feel I owe him a debt of gratitude. "

"I don't understand…"

"He made my life hell. I got strong because of it. I don't think I could have made it this long had it not been for him."

"I want so much to make it all up to you…" Mrs. Metcalf began, but Delse stopped her.

"Please … don't. It's hard enough for me just being here with you. Six months ago, I wouldn't have come, and to be honest I'm not sure why I'm here now."

Buried deep within her was a part of her that wanted to hurt this woman, to show her the pain she had caused and repay it somehow. However, closer to the surface was the need to know her, to love her and make up for all of the lost years between them, and this need was stronger.

"Sure, I've wondered about who you were and what you were like. Though never enough to search for you."

"Then why now?"

"A friend of mine is searching for her real parents. She came from the Forgiving Hearts

Orphanage, also. I guess I got caught up in it and decided to do the same."

"Well, whatever your motives were, I'm glad you're here now. Do you think you and I could ever be friends?"

"I think so." Delse rose to her feet and glanced toward the door. It was time for her to go. "I' m glad I came." And with that, she turned and started for the door.

"You can't stay awhile longer?"

"No, there's another storm coming and I really should be getting back," she said, putting on her coat.

"Can I call you sometime?"

"Yes … I'd like that."

There were tears in both their voices though Delse, a lifetime of practice behind her, hid hers better. Once again, silence ensued with each of them standing, staring, longing. It was Mrs. Metcalf who took the chance and threw her arms around Delse, holding on tightly.

Delse allowed her walls to slip, and now her tears flowed freely. Mother and daughter were reunited and somehow, as though by a miracle, a lifetime of hurt and of hate seemed distant and non-threatening.

"Will you join us for Christmas? I can't wait to show you off."

Delse was caught short. This was one thing she hadn't thought of happening. Her heart soared though she dared not show it, not yet. "Thank you … ma'am," she heard herself say. It sounded strange from her lips, somehow wrong. "I'd like that very much."

The door opened and Delse stepped through it. Gone again, only this time not for good. She would be back.

New tears sprang forth as Delse's mother gazed lovingly after her daughter and the wall of ice around her own heart began to melt. A new start had been offered to both of them and this time it wouldn't be wasted.

# CHAPTER 9

After Delse left to meet with her mother, Meagan had returned to the hotel and now found herself alone in her room.

Mike, who had clearly become more to Delse than she as letting on, and Bruce, who was getting nowhere with her case, were off somewhere playing pool. She had told them both to get out. She needed to think. Every lead had led to one more brick wall, but she felt there was something there. Something obscured in the mist … just out of reach. And she could see it if only she had peace and quiet to think.

Outside, the snow was falling again. It was hypnotic. Turning from the window back to the photocopied articles spread out on the table, Meagan once again began to read. Leaning back into her seat, she picked up the article on the fire and read slowly, going over every detail. There wasn't much there; in fact, it wasn't anything written in the article that had struck a chord as much as the photograph accompanying it. The picture was apparently a file photo taken when the orphanage had first started up operations.

Six people around the sign—at first she mused at how the styles had changed… and thank God. But then her gaze fell to the names listed below the picture. The print was very small and whatever process had been used to transfer the original to the micro phish had blurred many of the letters.

> SHOWN ABOVE IS THE STAFF OF THE FORGIVING
> HEARTS ORPHANAGE. FROM LEFT TO RIGHT
> THEY ARE: HELEN WINDSOR, STEPHEN BISHOP,
> KATHERINE MCDOUGAL, DANIEL LEAP, AND
> JACOB CARMICHAEL.

Daniel Leap! The old woman had lied to her. She said she had never spoken to anyone working at the orphanage. Meagan stared intently at the picture –more specifically at the young man holding a pipe standing second from the right. She recalled the empty pipe stand on Norma Leap's mantle.

What was it Delse had told her about a pipe? For the moment, the conversation was lost. It didn't matter. The old woman had knowingly deceived her, and now that left Meagan with unfinished business.

\*\*\*

An uneasiness crept over Meagan as she approached Norma Leap's driveway. The entrance to the Forgiving Hearts' drive was directly across the road, and seeing the ancient burned-out hulk seasoned by late-afternoon shadows made the entire scene appear diabolical.

Leap's house was set back from the road and, unlike her last visit, the lane hadn't been ploughed. Snow lay six inches deep the entire length of the drive. The house was small when compared to its closest neighbor and its white siding showed far too much of its age to be considered fashionable. Behind and off to the right of the house three weather-beaten barns sprang up from the snow. At least a dozen boards were missing from the largest of these and the darkened spaces that remained resembled the missing teeth of some horrible grey beast.

Meagan parked the car facing out of the bitter wind currently sweeping across the fields, and approached the screen porch.

This time the door opened without hesitation. Norma, recognizing Meagan's car as it came up the drive, was busying herself in the kitchen waiting for Meagan to appear at the door.

"Hello, Mrs. Leap," Meagan said as she was ushered in out of the darkening cold.

"Well, hello, dear," the old woman returned. "What brings you all the way out here on a night like this?"

"I have a few more questions for you, if that's all right?"

"Sure. That's fine. Good to have company round on nasty nights like this one." Meagan smiled, thinking, *it's about to get a whole lot nastier before it's over.*

"Now, dear, I've got the kettle all boiled up, but I forgot how you take your tea," Norma said apologetically.

"Black is fine."

"Good. Let's go in the den. I got a fire going."

Meagan followed Norma as she picked up the two cups and started off. A thin veil of smoke hung near the ceiling in the den, its odour mingling with the stale smell of the room.

"Okay now. You sit there, dear," Norma said, referring to the sofa. "And I'll sit here next to the fire … old bones, ya know."

Meagan smiled. Her mind whirled, searching for a tactful way of broaching the subject of Daniel Leap. However, after a number of various scenarios played themselves out in her head, she realized there was no tactful way.

"Who is Daniel Leap?"

The smile dropped from the old woman's face. Her eyes narrowed and somehow the whole bearing of the woman began to change.

"Daniel was my son," she replied. The friendliness so thick in her voice only an instant earlier was now gone.

"Was?"

"Yes. Was."

"So he's dead then?"

"Young lady, what business is that of yours?" Norma demanded.

"Because, Mrs. Leap, you lied to me when you said you hadn't spoken to anyone working over there."

"Ya, so what!"

"Well, I think you know a lot more than what you're letting on and I want to know why that is, Mrs. Leap."

"That's not your concern!" she hissed through her false teeth.

"Oh, that's alright. Here, I'll tell you what I've come up with. You see, I think your son Daniel was using those young girls over there for his own very unchristian devices…"

"No! Stop it! It's not true!" she sobbed "It's not true!"

"Oh, but I think it is true, and I also think you knew about it all along."

"No. No, I didn't!" Her denial halted. "How did you find out?"

"So I am right."

"Yes, my son Daniel was sick, but how did you know? Who told you?"

"You told me, ma'am."

"I did not!"

"Yes, ma'am, you did. When you told me that you had never spoken to anyone working over there it struck me as being odd, but I didn't say anything. Then I found this article with your son's picture where he's holding a pipe. The same pipe meant to sit in that pipe stand on the mantel piece."

"So, all that says is he worked there and I didn't tell ya."

"That's right, but you see, I also found an article about how three of the girls from over there went missing and were later found murdered. Now, when I realized that your son did indeed work there, I had to ask myself— why would you not want me to know about it unless you were too ashamed to tell me the truth?"

"It's time you were leaving," Norma hissed.

"The newspaper mentioned a fifth girl was unaccounted for after the fire. Was he responsible for that as well?" Meagan pressed.

"I said get out!"

***

The storms from the previous day had now continued on their way north along the coast of Lake Huron, leaving Sarnia to lavish in clear weather. Not many people visited the park along the river during the winter and so the snow was mostly unmarked by footprints, giving the appearance of purity.

The park bordered directly onto Sarnia Bay and now, with the water completely frozen over, Motocross wannabees were having a field day. The air was filled with the deep rumblings of them racing their noisy two-wheeled death traps in wide, crazed circles on the ice. Meagan watched in awe of them, sure that at any moment one would plunge through the ice into the unforgiving water hidden below. However, the likelihood of such an occurrence actually happening was far from the realm of possibilities. The ice here was far too thick—four feet in places.

Her journey to Sarnia had turned up nothing. She should have been grossly disappointed, but for reasons she was unable to explain, she was not. Hadn't all been for nothing, after all? The next time she saw Thorn she would tell him about Daniel Leap and then finally that case could be marked closed.

Delse was happy. She had found a whole host of people ready and willing to share in her life, not the least of which were her mother and Mike. In some ways, just knowing that Delse would be all right softened any disappointment Meagan might have otherwise felt. But then, Delse was a survivor and would have come out all right regardless of what had happened.

It was Julia she worried most for. She had taken this whole ordeal in ways no one could have foreseen and had allowed it to change her. Perhaps each of them had been changed by all that had happened, but none so much as Julia. Her spirit, it seemed, was broken. Her love of life had almost completely dwindled away to nothing, and she was left to deal with the shattered remnants of the life she once had. Meagan knew that what had happened to Julia was in part her fault. If she had never come here to Sarnia, perhaps none of it would have happened. Perhaps not, she told herself, but then so much had happened that it would have been difficult to say for certain.

It was time for her to leave, to return home to Collingwood and seek out the home and parents she already had there. She still believed that she had been perfectly justified in her quest and perhaps someday in the future she would pick it up again, but for now she conceded to the fact that it was over.

"Are you nuts?" Delse's voice drifted across the undisturbed snow. "You're going to freeze to death out here!"

"Hi, Delse."

"Hey, what's up? You look funny."Delse's concern was genuine, though her choice of words was typical of her usual flair for the language.

"Nothing's up. I think it's time I packed it in."

"Ah, come on, you've hardly given it a chance. Besides, you're probably still feeling bummed from your run-in with that old bag Norma Leap."

"No, Daniel Leap got what he deserved. And I *have* given it a chance. In fact, I've given it more than that." She sighed. "It's just not as important as it once was, you know?"

"Somebody slap me! I must be dreaming," Delse gasped. "You are the last person I thought I would ever see give up. Julia yes, but never you … what gives?"

"I told you, nothing. It's just time that I got my life back. For months, I've had everything on hold only to come up empty. The price was too high, Delse. Don't you see?"

"But what about the old lady and her goons in the limo?" Delse demanded. "You want to wait until the cops catch them, don't you?"

"No, the police can handle that."

"Well, what about me and Julia?" It was clear by this point that Delse was grasping for straws.

"You don't need me here. You never did. As for Julia, well, I don't think she wants either of us around right at the moment, if you know what I mean."

Meagan turned back toward the bay. Her mind was made up.

# CHAPTER 10

"Julia, run! Run faster, he's right behind you... run!"

She was five years old again. Her tiny legs pounded out each increasingly painful stride. She glanced quickly over her shoulder. No one was there.

Why was she running, and from what?

The day would come when she would leave this place. She couldn't wait. Dark shadows loomed everywhere. Each of them holding a new threat, promising new horrors ...

"Julia," he whispered darkly. Oh no, he had found her. The air filled with the aroma of pipe smoke.

"Julia," came the whisper again.

*Where is he?* her mind screamed. *I can't see him.*

"Julia!"

"Julia! Wake up. Tommy's been taken to St. Joseph's!" Susan's tone was filled with urgency.

"What? What happened?" Julia demanded, coming to life behind her desk and immediately jumping to her feet.

"Seems one of his mother's boyfriends needed a punching bag. Come on, we should be there."

Nothing more needed to be said. Julia, her coat slung across her shoulders, was already racing for the door. This was her fault, she told herself. She had been there only yesterday and could have easily prevented this from happening. Instead, she had done nothing and now Tommy was lying the St. Joseph's emergency room.

"This is my fault, Sue," Julia said as they made their way toward the car.

"Bullshit. How could you have prevented something like this? After all, you can't be there twenty-four hours of the day," Susan snapped.

"I was there yesterday. I was going to pull him!" she wailed. "Damn it, Sue, I chickened out! I didn't even go inside because I knew what I'd find if I did. And then I'd have no choice but to pull him!"

"Don't beat yourself up over something that's done. Let's just go and pick up the pieces."

"What about the boyfriend? Do the police have a description?" Julia demanded.

"No need. He's dead."

"What! How the hell did that happen?"

"Tommy's mother shot him." Susan's voice was cold, full of the detachment Julia had once found so difficult to muster. "She's in custody up on manslaughter charges."

"It's about time the stupid bitch did something for Tom!" Julia spat.

"I hope you're not telling me that you condone what she did?" Susan's eyes widened as she glanced over to taste Julia's reaction.

"No, of course not," Julia said. She was lying. "I'm saying that I'm glad she finally did something unselfish on the boy's behalf."

"That's what I thought," Susan affirmed. She was not totally buying into Julia's explanation, but it would have to do for now.

Conversation dwindled as Susan brought the car to a stop in the emergency room parking area. There had to be fifteen signs posted conspicuously, all proclaiming that unauthorized vehicles would be towed at the owner's expense. Neither of them took the slightest notice as they left the car at a run and darted through the automated doors to the reception desk.

"Hello, my name is Susan Grant and this is Julia Hart. We're with the Children's Aid Society and we've come to see Thomas Mitchell. He was just brought in."

From behind her glass partition, the weathered nurse eyed their credentials with dull scrutiny before speaking. "Have a seat. I'll inform the doctor you're here."

"You don't understand," Julia piped up. "We would like to see him now."

"Sorry, sweetie," the nurse said. "That isn't possible. The doctor is in with him now.

Please have a seat and I will tell him you're here."

"Who authorized the treatment?" Susan demanded. "Why, the boy's mother of course."

Both requests to see him fell upon deaf ears, leaving them no choice but to comply with the nurse's instructions and take a seat. Time passed slowly. Their eyes were glued to the dozen or so closed doors leading from the sterile corridor into the treatment rooms, searching for any sign of one of them opening. For the longest time, there was nothing. No indication at all, and the nurse, so persistent that she would inform the doctor of their arrival, had yet to move from her perch behind the partition.

"God, this is maddening!" Julia growled. "What could be taking so long?"

"Maybe he was hurt more severely than we were led to believe."

"I hope not..." Julia's thought was cut short as one of the doors finally opened and out stepped a tall, grey-haired doctor wearing blood-stained surgical garb.

Like a shot, Julia was on her feet and moving to intercept the doctor before he could disappear into yet another treatment room.

"Miss! You can't go in there!" protested the nurse from behind the partition. Julia ignored her.

"Doctor, my name is Julia Hart and I'm with Children's Aid. Thomas Mitchell is one of my kids. Is he going to be all right?"

"You say he's one of your kids? Well, not anymore he isn't."

"What are you saying?" Susan, who had joined Julia, demanded.

From behind, the determined squelch resounded from the nurse's rubber-soled shoes
as she stormed forward to claim her quarry. "Doctor, I tried to stop them but them..."

"Don't worry about it, nurse. Please just return to your station and I'll take it from here," he instructed before turning his attention back to Julia and Susan.

"I'm certain the two of you can prove that you are who you say?"

"Of course we can!" Susan stated, thrusting her identification forward, followed in rapid succession by Julia. "Now, what did you mean by he isn't one of our kids any longer?"

"Just that. Thomas Mitchell just died of massive internal injuries. We just couldn't stop the bleeding," the doctor said.

128

Moments later a sheet-draped stretcher was wheeled past them and down the hall.

"That can't be. For Christ sake, what kind of a hospital is this, anyway?" Julia demanded. "The kid was beat up. He wasn't hit by a fucking Mack truck!" Julia's face was reddening at an alarming rate.

"Listen, lady, I do my best to save the ones I can. I do my job. Perhaps if you people did yours a little better I'd see fewer broken bodies like Thomas Mitchell's!" His retort stung deep, striking Julia silent.

"Now, you'll have to excuse me. I have other patients to attend to." He left them standing there as he walked into the next treatment room.

Nothing remained to be done, nothing to be said. And for a fleeting second, a thought dashed across a shadowy corner of Julia's mind … perhaps it was better this way. For now, he wouldn't have to deal with the pain and guilt this life so amply provided. A convenient lie, she told herself, nothing more.

Inside her, something was different. Something dreadful was taking place and she was helpless to prevent it. Her heart was hardening, obstructing the tears, due Tommy's death, to flow. She doubted if tears would ever come again.

\*\*\*

Leaving her car, Julia started across the icy parking lot toward her apartment building. Susan had given her an extended Christmas holiday to get herself together, but she doubted it would help. *Christmas*, she thought, *what a joke that was*. A time for love, for giving and receiving—it wouldn't be that way for her this year. All that was now a thing of the past for her and she really wasn't looking forward to this one.

Her failure with Tommy, coupled with everything else that had happened recently, had sealed it better than any glue known to man.

The parking lot to her building was busy at the best of times. And so she initially took little notice of the car as it drew to a halt a short distance away. Even less did she notice the young man wearing the long grey overcoat getting out of the back seat and moving toward the front entrance of the building.

Deciding against taking the stairs, she emerged into the main hall from the side entrance and approached the elevator. The young man from the parking lot was already standing there waiting and she simply stepped up beside him and joined in the wait.

His back was turned to her, hiding his face, but then, she saw this as nothing to be concerned about. After all, many business men lived in the building—most of them being quite harmless. She had no reason to suspect anything different from this one. So as the doors parted and he stepped aboard, she followed without apprehension.

"What floor?" he asked, still not allowing her to see his face.

"Third," he responded. Elevator conversation was sporadic at best. Reaching for the panel, he paused over the third-floor button and pressed seven instead.

The doors closed.

"No, you got it wrong. I said the third floor." Her tone sounded slightly annoyed by the blunder.

He said not a word, though now he turned to face her, and as he did her eyes widened. Shock, surprise and wonderment at her own stupidity all came flooding together, pushing aside any other emotion there previously.

"You don't make it easy, Miss Hart. You should be more considerate toward the needs of others," he intoned.

"Are you out of your fucking head? Stop this elevator at once, before I scream my head off!" she barked back, clearly in no mood for this.

"Sorry. I can't do that. But then, you knew that, right?" From his pocket, he eased a white piece of cloth folded into a three-inch square and took a step forward.

"Hey now, come on. That shit gave me one hell of a headache last time. I'd rather you didn't use it."

"Shut up, bitch!" With that, he lunged, but having anticipated this move, Julia threw herself out of the way, if only momentarily. "Elevators aren't a great place to try to run in, you know?" He sneered and came at her again. This time he grabbed her by the throat and pressed the cloth heavily over her nose and mouth. Desperately, she resisted the urge to breath.

With the chloroform stinging her eyes and burning the interior passages of her nose, she was fading. She would have to breathe soon, but she had to time it right.

The numbered lights over the elevator door had just lit six and any second would hit seven. *It has to be now,* she told herself. A terrible numbing was setting in. It had to be now! Now!

The elevator lugged to a halt and as it did she raised her knee with all the might her now semi-conscious mind could muster.

It was enough. He doubled over and as the doors parted she gave him one last vicious shove and leapt for freedom.

There was no time to try summoning help from behind one of the closed apartment doors—he was already getting up.

The stairs!

The stairs were her only hope. Now if only she could get enough of a head start to make them work to her advantage.

Her eyes watering badly as the last vestiges of the chloroform's effect slowly subsided, she ran virtually blind to the end of the hall and the door to her escape.

The stairs were wet from the constant tracking of snow-laden boots, making her rapid descent all the more difficult. Half running, half falling, she urged her body downward, certain that he was right behind her and bent on capture. She didn't turn to look— that would have been taking too great a risk.

Suddenly, the slamming sound of a heavy metal fire door leading from one of the floors filled the air and echoed deceivingly through the chimney-like stairwell.

It chilled her blood with the knowledge he was now getting closer— but had the door slammed behind her or in front? She had no real way of knowing for certain. She could only hope it came from behind and continue her mad, unseeing descent.

All at once some absurd little voice inside of her head began screaming at her that something was wrong … something was missing. Resisting her every primal instinct, she slowed to a stop and listened.

Soon she knew what was missing. There were no footfalls. He wasn't coming after her. He was waiting!

Her heart pounding at a fever pitch, her tortured breath burning within her aching chest, she chanced a look over the side of the banister. At first, nothing appeared threatening below. Then, out of the corner of her eye, she caught the slight movement of a shadow on the landing three floors below. He was waiting. She had almost run right into him. *How could you be so stupid*, she scolded herself and immediately began inching her way back to the fifth-floor fire door.

Her every movement seemed to echo out loudly as seconds ticked passed with agonizing sluggishness. Easing the door open slightly—just wide enough to allow her body through—she slipped into the hall and once again broke into a dead run.

Now the heavy pounding of his footfalls could be heard echoing in the stairwell as, realizing he had been discovered, he wasted no energy in an attempt for silence.

Frantically, Julia punched the elevator buttons, praying that one would respond in time. He was getting closer. Behind the steel elevator doors, the whirr of wires and motors bringing the coach slowly upward frustrated her.

Again, she pressed the buttons.

There was a thud followed by a slight gasp and the doors began to part. She squeezed between them when they were still only twelve inches apart and immediately began pressing the button to close the doors again. She didn't realize that for the button to work, the doors had to first come all the way open.

At the end of the hall, the door leading from the stairs flung open and through it leapt the man in the grey overcoat. He could hear the elevator doors closing, and though winded from his ascent of six flights, he raced toward it.

Too late.

The doors closed seconds before he arrived. Julia Hart was gone.

The immediate danger now past, Julia allowed her knees to buckle and her body to slide slowly down the elevator wall. Her head tilted back, her mind still reeling as to what her next course of action would be once the elevator reached the first floor. Surely he would be there waiting. One thing in her favour was she knew he probably didn't want to harm her. No, the old lady would have his hide if he were to do anything like that.

Her eyes were peeled on the lit numbers over the door, and no plan of attack was coming clear in her mind. Perhaps she should just bolt through the doors when they opened and hope for the best. It sounded lame, sure it did, but then she had no weapons and only herself to rely on.

Silently, she found herself wishing that Delse were there. She would know what to do, and even if she didn't she would certainly be able to fight her way through. The first floor was approaching rapidly, and as it did, all fantasies of Delse coming to her rescue faded as the reality of her situation settled home. The doors opened and Julia burst into the hall, running right into the arms of Constable Thorn.

"Julia, what's the rush?" he asked, setting her back on her own feet.

"The limo…" she gasped. "…the limo driver just tried to grab me again. I left him on the fifth floor."

"I wouldn't worry about him. I have four of my best men combing the building for him right now," he said to reassure her. "Come on, I'll buy you a drink and you can tell me all about what happened here today."

"Wait … what are you doing here? How did you know?"

"Let's just say I've been keeping an eye on you."

Julia could shake the creepiness of Thorn's last statement, but allowed herself to be led from the building.

# CHAPTER 11

"Still no answer at Julia's place?" Delse asked, entering the room.

Meagan simply shook her head, listening as Julia's phone rang for the ninth time. "I don't get it. Her boss said she went home early. Something to do with losing one of her kids,"

"Well, I wouldn't lose sleep over it if I were you. After all, she wasn't the friendliest when she was here last."

"Oh, I see, and for that we should shut her out, is that it?" Meagan snarled.

"I didn't say that. What I meant was she's probably not answering her phone because she's thinking it's us trying to call," Delse explained.

"Delse, she's a bitch. She's not psychic!"

"Oh yeah, sorry, lost my head." Delse shrugged. "Why is it so important that you talk to her anyway?"

"Because last time she was here she seemed weird, that's all. I'm a bit concerned."

"Well, I always thought she was weird. But if you're that worried, why don't we drive over there and make sure she's all right?" Delse offered

"You wouldn't mind?"

"Hell, no. Besides, it'll give her another crack at insulting our intelligence," Delse resigned with a slight smile. "Come on, you're driving."

The day was wearing on when they left Delse's apartment and started making their way across town. Almost four-thirty and the traffic was heavy, making driving the slushy streets dangerous.

As a precaution, Meagan eased up on the gas a little— much to Delse's displeasure—increasing their travelling time by about ten minutes.

Twenty minutes later, Delse and Meagan stood side by side next to Julia's car. Using a trick she once saw in a movie, Delse placed her hand on the hood to see if it had been there long. The hood was cold. Clearly the car had been sitting there for quite some time.

"Well, she's been here for a while." Delse stated. "Come on, let's go try the buzzer."

Upon arriving at the front of the building they found the controlled entrance barred open by a wooden doorstop.

"Lordy! A crook could have a field day with the security in this joint," Delse teased, while Meagan buzzed Julia's apartment for the third time. Again, there was no response to the summons.

"Maybe she went out on a date or something?" Meagan rationalized.

"You have got to be kidding. Miss-Stuck-Up-Blond? Please!"

"Will you ease up on her a little? Come on, let's try knocking on her door."

"Must be that time of the month— no sense of haw-haw," Delse murmured.

"I heard that, Miss Collier," Meagan scolded, only half serious.

"Sorry, Mom," Delse returned mockingly.

Delse hated elevators and grew increasing more nervous as the coach jolted and lugged between floors. She began to fidget, examining the numbers over the doors, the control panel, and the broken strap on her right boot. It was then that she noticed the key ring in the corner of the elevator.

"Some unlucky stiff lost his keys," she observed, bending down to retrieve them. Turning them over in her hand and finding nothing of interest, she pocketed them.

Much to Delse's delight the elevator stopped, the doors opened and they were free of it.

Julia lived in apartment 310 located at the end of the hall next to the fire exit. Meagan was the first to arrive at the door, and she knocked smartly.

No response.

Delse, having grown bored, took out the keys and began fumbling with them again, only this time she noticed something she hadn't before. One of the keys was stamped with the numbers 3-1-0.

"Meagan, look at this," she said, holding up the key in question.

Meagan's brow immediately furrowed with worry as she snatched the keys from Delse's hand and inserted the one marked 310 into the lock. It fit.

"I really don't like the way this is feeling," Meagan intoned, pushing the door and stepping slowly inside. Delse's boredom forgotten, she prepared herself for anything as they slowly crept around the empty apartment.

There was nothing to indicate that Julia had been back since leaving for work earlier that morning. On the dining room table was a plate with a half-eaten piece of burnt toast and an empty coffee cup. Surely, if she had returned after leaving work she would have cleared these things away, Meagan told herself silently.

"What do you think happened?" Delse asked dumbly.

"I have no idea. One thing's for certain, though, I don't buy the date idea anymore."

"What, then? The limo driver?"

"Maybe..." All at once Meagan seemed a thousand miles away. "Where are the guys?"

"Don't know. Those two have really hit it off since she kicked them out of my place the other day. They're probably out playing pool somewhere. You know, that whole male bounding thing. Want me to track them down?"

"No, don't worry about it. I think we should call the police and get Constable Thorn up here right away."

An unusual feeling numbed Meagan's fingers as she dialed the number of the police station. Perhaps they were making more out of this than it truly deserved; after all, Julia hadn't been all that generous when it came to offering details about her plans and whereabouts. For all they knew she might have gone back to London to be with her parents. The suitcases still in her closet told them that wasn't the case.

The phone rang twice before a pleasant-sounding woman picked up. "Sarnia-Clearwater Police Department, how may I direct your call?"

"Constable Thorn, please."

"I'm sorry, miss, but there is no one by that name here. Perhaps you've got the name wrong. May I forward your call to one of the officers on duty?"

"When does Thorn come back on duty?" Meagan pressed.

"No, ma'am, you don't understand. There is no such person as Constable Thorn working out of this department."

"How can that be? I've spoken to the man myself."

"I really don't know what to tell you, ma'am."

"You're certain this person called himself Constable Thorn?"

"Yes! He was supposed to investigating a triple kidnapping complaint involving myself and two others."

"Let me switch you to the duty sergeant." Without waiting for Meagan to reply, the call was transferred and male voice came onto the line.

By this time, however, Meagan was struck silent as the implications of what she had just learned sunk home.

"Hello, is there someone there?" asked the male voice. "Hello?"

Meagan slowly returned the receiver to its cradle and turned to Delse, who was watching Meagan's horrified expression with one of her own.

"I'm not going to like this, am I?" Delse said cautiously.

Meagan shook her head. "We've been had. There is no such person as a Constable Thorn in the SarniaClearwater Police Department."

"That's impossible. Bruce introduced him to us."

"Yeah, I know."

"You don't think Bruce is trying to screw us around too, do you?"

"I hope not. But before I make a call on that one, I think we should have a chat with our Mr. Bruce Stewart." Meagan's tone sounded ominous.

"Do you have even the slightest idea where we'd find them?"

"Only a guess, but they have been spending a lot of time down at Vices. We could start there."

"Okay, let's go take a look."

Vices was a place aptly named, in Meagan's opinion. The room was dark, though not dark enough to hide a large bloodstain on the carpet to the left of the bar, nor did it hide the strippers seated provocatively on stools skirting its length. Along the walls, pool tables highlighted by low-hanging swag lamps filled the air with hollow-sounding thumps signifying yet another successful shot.

Off to the left of the door as they came in was a table of seven grossly over-weight men and women, though to distinguish between them, Meagan would have been hard pressed. There could have been little doubt in the minds of those watching her walk in at Delse's side that she did not belong there.

"Hey, Delse, feel like giving a few lessons today?" called out a tall balding man with a pot belly seated at the bar.

"Hank, I told ya already. I don't give lessons to losers. Besides, you're one of my best pigeons."

"Delse, cool it!" Meagan whispered nervously.

"Will you relax a little? No one's going to mess with ya, I'll see to it," she said confidently.

"Great ... I feel so much better," Meagan quipped as they moved deeper into the darkened bar.

"Come on, there's the guys," Delse stated. Sure enough, there at the back table Bruce and Mike were circling their shots like hungry sharks. "You go on over. There's something I have to do first." Meagan hesitated. "Go on, will you!" Delse pushed. "I'll be over in a second."

"Hi guys," Meagan said, trying to act calm. "Bruce, I hope I' m not paying for this."

"Meagan, darling, you haven't been paying since the kidnapping. Nope, that made it personal."

"Well, my wallet thanks you for that. Come on," she said as she grabbed the cue ball from the table and started toward a booth.

"Hey, Meagan, what gives?" Mike protested.

"Get over here and I'll tell you." She had the cue ball, leaving them little choice but to do as they were told.

"Where's Delse?" Mike asked suspiciously as he climbed into the booth.

"She'll be along in a moment."

"Okay, Meg, let's have it. What's up?" Bruce asked.

"Julia's gone," Meagan began.

"So what. She never tells anyone what she's doing. Probably just went back to London or something," Mike offered.

"Yeah, or something... listen, will you? Her car is still in the parking lot of her building. We found these in the elevator." She threw the keys onto the table. "And she hasn't been back to her apartment since leaving for work this morning. At first we thought, like you, that maybe she had a date or went back to London, but it doesn't make sense that she didn't take her car and when we found her keys ..."

"You think it's the limo driver again?" Mike asked.

"Did you call Thorn?" Bruce added before she could respond to Mike's questions.

"That's the other thing ... there's no such person. The police department here has never even heard of a Constable Thorn." The tone of accusation was heavy in her voice, drawing a suspicious glance from Mike.

By this point, Delse had returned with news of her activities. "The cops may not have heard of Thorn, but the word down here is that he's a hired gun. He's supposedly working for some rich dame. Ring any bells?" Delse offered.

"Wait a second here, I spoke to the guy!" Bruce protested. "Fucker was there when I woke up in the hospital."

"That means we were right. She does have Julia again," Meagan exclaimed, ignoring Bruce's insistence.

"That's right."

"So where do we look? They could have taken her anywhere," Mike stated.

"No, not anywhere. If Thorn is not a cop, as is becoming clear he isn't, I say we start with the mansion where you girls were held the first time," Bruce said, eyeing the others for traces of disbelief. There were none.

"Shouldn't we contact the real police before we try something like that?" Meagan warned.

"And what will they do?" Delse barked. "Julia's not a minor and it hasn't been forty-eight hours since she went missing ... they won't touch this."

"No, Delse ... Meagan's right. We just have to come up with a way to convince them. Leave that to me," Bruce offered.

"Right now, I think the rest of you should get out there."

"Agreed," Delse stated. "Let's go."

Twenty minutes later Meagan and Delse rode shotgun out of town with Mike in the cab of his truck while Bruce made his way to the police station.

It wasn't going to be an easy task getting the police to listen. Bruce knew this for a fact. He had dealt with the police before, largely due his sister's unfortunate choice of a husband, only to find their policies far too rigid to be useful in times such as this. Unfortunately, he wouldn't be able to use sisterly blackmail this time to get his way. Still, the truth would be of no use to him—well, perhaps not the whole truth, especially if he was to get their cooperation.

"The captain will see you now, Mr. Stewart," said a smiling attractive young woman in uniform.

"Thank you," he replied as he rushed past her into the office.

"Mr. Stewart, how may I help you today? All I ask is that you make this fast. I have a very busy afternoon," intoned the captain.

"Well, sir, it's about to get a whole lot busier ..."

Bruce went on to tell the captain about the first kidnapping, the phony Constable Thorn and then the most recent disappearance of Julia Hart. Of course, he exaggerated wherever possible to make their plight seem more urgent to the captain. And from the look upon his face it appeared his bid was successful.

"That's quite a tale," the captain began. "And you never once thought to ask to see this man's identification?" He smirked.

Bruce knew what was behind the smirk. He had dealt with the condescending police opinion of private investigators his entire career. This was nothing new.

"No, of course not ..." Bruce explained. "After all, the first time I ever laid eyes on the guy, I was barely conscious in the hospital following the kidnapping of Meagan Bathurst, and he was introduced to me as Constable Thorne by the doctor whose care I was under."

"I see, and now you believe that this woman, Julia Hart, has been taken again by these same people?"

"Yes, sir, I do. Not only that, but we believe ..."

"Who's this we?"

"Myself, Delse Collier, Meagan Bathurst and Mike Grey. Captain, we're wasting time here! Right at this very moment Mike, Delse and Meagan are on their way out to that house to rescue Julia. You have to get some of your people on this and fast!"

"I don't have to do anything, mister!" It was clear that the captain was not the sort who liked being told what his job entailed. Bruce decided to use a different tact.

"It would be horrible if those people out there got themselves injured while you just sat here knowing all along what they were up to, wouldn't it?" Bruce slimed. "I mean, think of what the local papers could do with a story like that. The possibilities are almost endless."

"Mr. Stewart!" the captain barked. "I do believe you're threatening me!"

"Who can say for certain, you know? I mean, the line between a threat and a promise is so very thin, after all." The captain's eyes widened noticeably.

Bruce Stewart wasn't backing down. It was a characteristic he was altogether not used to when people addressed him. "What do you say, Captain? Do I get some help here or will the papers get one hell of a story?"

"You'll get the help you need. Hold on for a minute, though, you'll have to ride with one of the officers and show my people the way."

"I'd be more than happy to do that little thing for you, Captain. When do we leave?"

"Right now, but I'll tell you this. There had better be something out there or you will be one less Dick bringing down the neighborhood."

"See what I mean, Captain, such thin lines."

Mike's rig jostled along old highway #7 past the spot where he first found the girls. He was figuring they would then take it from there and locate the house by retracing their steps. All in all, it shouldn't prove to be difficult, he thought. Both Delse and Meagan seemed confident they could find the house again.

"Okay, stop the truck," Delse said.

"What? Why?" Mike queried.

Meagan picked it up from there. "We're going to get out here and go on foot. The house is roughly half a mile further up. You can't miss it; it's the only one there."

"How much insurance do you have on this rig of yours, Mike?" Delse asked.

"Enough, why?"

"Because we're going to need a diversion," she explained.

"Wonderful. Hey…your foot."

"I'll live."

"Give us fifteen minutes to get near the wall and then let her rip," Meagan said.

"You two watch too much television," he protested. "What happens if it doesn't work?"

"Mike, make it work. Stop worrying. You're worse than an old lady sometimes."

"Thank you, thank you very much, Delse. I needed that."

"Love you, babe," she replied, kissing him warmly before getting down from the cab.

"Wait, what?" He was stunned

"Okay, now remember, fifteen minutes," Meagan reminded him, and with that the two of them set off through the brush toward the wall.

He watched them go, thinking the whole time that he must be crazy for allowing anything so completely halfcocked. However, the time for debating the issue had long since gone. Now it was up to him to ensure they didn't get their asses kicked.

"Did she say she loved me?" he asked himself aloud.

He smiled.

The minutes ticked past.

The compound was closer than they first thought and they reached the wall with five minutes to spare. However, Delse wasn't concerned over this. They would be able to use the time by sizing up the grounds on the other side of the wall. Perhaps even getting closer to the house before Mike made his grand entrance.

"Now what?" Meagan said, standing thigh-deep in drifted snow.

"We take a look, what else?"

"I think we should wait for Mike!" Meagan protested.

"He'll be there. Come on."

" 'I love you, babe?' " Meagan mocked.

"Oh, for shit sakes, not now. Give me a boost. I want to see what we're up against."

"Delse, sometimes you are a royal pain in the ass, do you know that?"

"Yes, thank you. Now give me a hand!"

It was lucky for Meagan that Delse only weighed one hundred and ten pounds, because the ground below the drift was uneven at best, making an already awkward situation seem worse.

"Can you see anything?" Meagan groaned.

"Yeah, plenty," came the reply.

The grounds beyond the wall were a veritable maze of shrubs and neatly trimmed evergreens. Up next to the house a large swimming pool seemed to extend out from inside a dome-shaped, tinted glass enclosure. The water of the pool hadn't been winterized, so it was sending up a dancing layer of steam clinging to the surface of the water, telling Delse that the water was heated and most likely the pool was used all year round. Extending back from the house along the far left of the compound was another large building—probably a parking garage. Next to it was yet another building, though this one was much smaller and most likely used for grounds equipment storage. One thing Delse found surprising was the total absence of activity beyond the wall. Nothing moved there; there weren't even dogs visible.

"Okay, bring me down."

"My pleasure," Meagan said in compliance. "So, what's in there?"

"Lots of good cover and no one to get in our way, but we'll have to move carefully. Never know who might be looking out one of those windows," Delse cautioned. "Come on, we'll use that tree to help us get over the wall," she added, referring to a stunted poplar standing a few feet from the wall.

"I really think we should wait for Mike."

"Yeah, well, you worry too much. Besides, we only have a couple minutes left before he does whatever it is he's planning to do."

Without further debate, they mounted the tree and soon were on the other side of the wall moving cautiously, shielded by hedge rows, toward the side wall of the parking structure. To this point it had been easy. Some might have insisted it had been too easy, though neither pondered its validity.

"Okay, last time we were here I couldn't see the pool so we were probably being held in a side room," Delse deduced.

"Makes sense."

"Come on," Delse prompted, and they were on the move again. This time they moved behind the smaller buildings to remain hidden from anyone looking out of a window in the main house.

The clock was running down. Soon Mike would be causing his diversion, allowing them to get into the house undetected.

A wooden side door exposed itself to them as they emerged from behind the garage. Probably a servant's entrance, Delse assumed.

"Okay, sit tight. There's our way in. Now all we have to do is wait for Mike."

Meagan nodded her agreement and the two slipped silently back under the cover of shadow.

The time had come, he told himself, and soon the air was filled with the roar of the massive diesel engine stoking up. The house was less than half a mile down the road—not a lot of space to climb through the gears, but he knew of a way.

The truck leapt from its mark and barreled forward like something possessed by demons. Mike worked the gears relentlessly, urging the screaming hulk of shining metal and smoking rubber to ever-greater speeds. The wall came quickly into view, followed in rapid succession by the iron gate.

"So much for the insurance rates!" he screamed, gearing higher and veering toward the gate.

Ice, snow and concrete dust filled the air as both pillars exploded in a barrage of shattered brick and twisted metal. The ground shook with the force of an atomic blast as the truck, moving far too fast at this point to stop, continued at breakneck speed toward the front door of the huge house.

"Holy shit! This one's gonna hurt!" he cried out and braced up hard for the coming impact.

Two guards who had witnessed the gate crashing raced for the front door and arrived in time to see the wall before them disintegrate and the demonic nose of the semi come crashing through. Neither guard would ever have to worry about seeing anything ever again. Both lay dead amidst the rubble.

The truck finally came to rest at the base of the spiral staircase.

Mike slumped partially conscious over the wheel, his face strewn with his own blood from a large gash in his forehead.

Meagan and Delse, who had leapt into action the instant the truck hit the gate, checked on Mike and then made their way up the stairs. On the first landing, a small table supporting a two-foot iron statue seemed strangely out of place from the scene only twelve feet below.

"That was some diversion," Meagan gasped, dumbfounded, as she followed Delse up the stairs while still looking back over the devastation.

"Yes, well, only the best for our Julia," Delse returned.

Delse stopped, and for a moment Meagan was puzzled, but soon saw the reason. A large man stood menacingly on the next landing, clearly in no mood for witty repartee. Meagan swallowed hard.

The fun was over.

Somehow they had to get past this hulking man to get to Julia and somehow Meagan just knew that he aimed to prevent it.

"Come on, you little fuckin' bitches. You just try to get past me."

"Okay, fuck nuts, let's party!" Delse screeched, taking on an aggressive stance. Meagan glanced around frantically for something, anything, that could be used as a weapon.

Delse produced one of her own design—an eight-inch switchblade.

Meagan watched in horror as Davey and Goliath squared off and approached one another. Delse held the knife, sharp side out, ready to swipe without warning. The man wasn't armed, but by sheer size clearly had the advantage. Throwing off her horror, Meagan used the distraction to slip back to the first landing and retrieve the statue. If he got past Delse, she was going to need something.

From the corner of her eye, Delse noted Meagan's return with the statue in hand. A plan formulated feverously in her mind. She could only hope that Meagan would pick up on what it was she was up to. Like a flash, Delse lashed out, lancing her blade across her opponent's abdomen, while in the same instant she lunged forward, and, taking advantage of his momentary loss of balance, pulled viciously at his shirt. The ploy worked. Their aggressor stumbled toward Meagan, who, more out of reflex than planned attack, swung the metal statue like a home-run-hitter. It connected with a bone-cracking thud, sending him crashing through the oak banister to join his to comrades on the rubble heap twenty-eight feet below.

"Nice hit, slugger!" Delse admired, picking herself up from the stairs and closing the knife.

"Yeah, it was, wasn't it? And they said playing tennis would never pay off." She grimaced.

"Come on, let's keep going."

"Do you think he's dead?"

Delse cast a backward glance over the railing at the unmoving man below. "Yup. You're a murderer. Let's go"

Soon they reached the top of the stairs and moved swiftly toward the room where they were all held the last time they visited.

"They wouldn't be stupid enough to keep her in the same room," Meagan said, still holding the statue.

"Why not? If Thorn's in on this, no one knows they're even here," Delse explained.

Silence overtook them as they approached the door to the room. No sound came from within, but they felt certain this was, in fact, the right one.

The door was locked. Without a moment's pause, Delse reached into her back pocket and removed a small leather case. In it were several instruments resembling partially straightened paper clips. Selecting two, she knelt down before the door and went to work on the lock.

"Where did you learn to do that?" Meagan asked.

"Don't ask so many questions," Delse warned, and moments later the lock tumbled free in the chamber.

Julia's eyes darted frantically about the room. She was clearly very upset. But then, who wouldn't have been in a similar situation? Meagan closed the door behind them and then all at once it became clear what Julia was trying to convey.

"Do come in, ladies," came the voice of Thorn as he emerged from behind a dressing screen. In his right hand was a rather ugly-looking snub-nosed revolver.

"Hello, Thorn. We were wondering when you'd make your appearance."

"Meagan, darling, you're not surprised to see me?"

"Should I be?" She laughed. "It wasn't hard at all to figure you into this." Ignoring the gun, she moved to Julia and removed her gag and untied her hands.

"Where's the old witch?" Delse demanded.

"Here I am, my dear," the old woman announced, emerging from behind the screen. "Now really, did you have to destroy my home?" she went on. "Oh, that's right. Your breeding. You couldn't help yourself."

This time Delse would not be silenced by her comments of breeding and social graces. "Cram it, you old bitch! I've had about all I'm going to take of your bullshit!"

"Delse, there are three guards in the house!" Julia cautioned.

"Not any more there aren't." Meagan smirked.

"Oh dear. You children really are a disgrace. I'm ashamed that one of you might actually have my blood in your veins."

"I would think you would be proud of them," Julia began. "They out-foxed an old pro like you. In my book that's something to be proud of."

"Yes, yes. You're all wonderful and if this totally enlightening conversation is complete, we should get a move on." Thorn, growing impatient, prompted.

"Quite right," agreed the old lady.

"First, Meagan, put down the statue and Delse, hand over the knife."

"Chuck-you-Farley! You come and get it," Delse instructed, launching the blade from its casing.

"Do it, now! If you don't, I'll just kill you now instead of later. The choice is yours."

"Delse, do as he says," Julia urged.

"Yeah, I think he means it," Meagan agreed, setting aside the statue.

"Damn straight."

Reluctantly, Delse closed the knife and tossed it to him.

"Now, move it, downstairs!" he instructed. "We're all going to take a car ride together."

Thorn and the old woman followed Julia and the others from the room and down the stairs. Julia's mouth was agape. She couldn't believe the amount of destruction. Strangely, there was something almost funny about seeing the huge semi in the entrance hall.

Picking their way through the rubble around the front of the truck, Delse glanced up into the cab. It was empty. Mike had recovered, hopefully enough to get them out of this, she prayed. Still, there was no sign of him anywhere.

# CHAPTER 12

"Nobody's here, Captain. Just the three stiffs in the hall," announced a newly appointed constable accompanied by two others who were equally as fresh. "Looks like someone was held against their will in the upstairs bedroom, though."

"Okay, thanks. Call it in," replied the captain, before turning to Bruce. "Okay, so you were right. Nobody's home— now what?"

"Beats hell out of me. We didn't plan on anything like this. They were supposed to be here."

"Think, for Christ's sake. Where else might they have gone? You know these people ... where?"

"I told you, I don't know!" Bruce exclaimed, but no sooner were the words past his lips when a thought began to form. "Wait a second. Wait one God damn second! The orphanage!"

"What orphanage?"

"The Forgiving Hearts, that's what orphanage. That's where this whole damned thing started. The old broad might have taken them out there."

"Now I know you're loony. That place burned down years ago," the captain said.

"I know, but the other buildings on the property are still standing. Come on, Captain, it has to be worth a look."

"I agree. Okay, give me minute." With that, the captain left to speak with a couple of his men. One was to remain there and wait for the coroner while the other two rookies were to come along to the orphanage as backup.

Minutes later they were underway.

Meagan and the others were directed to the entrance of a storm cellar that had gone unnoticed on Meagan's last visit.

The snow was drifted deeply over the slanted doors; clearly no one had been down there for quite some time. Then again, it might have only been since the last snow. She found it difficult to judge. The snow drifted constantly out here.

Had this been Collingwood, she would have been able to tell in a second, but it wasn't.

Perhaps it was solely because of their dire situation, perhaps it was something more, but she longed to be back there in that tiny town surrounded by water and mountains, three hundred and fifty miles to the north. So much could have been different. If only she had been satisfied with the life she had instead of searching for one that probably didn't even exist. She had hurt so many people, not the least of these Tina and Craig. She didn't blame herself, though, for what

was happening now. No, Delse and Julia and perhaps even herself would have been abducted whether or not she had come to Sarnia, and she was glad not to have to face it alone.

Thorn finished clearing the snow away and lifted the ancient wooden doors.

The doors open, Meagan, Delse, and Julia were directed inside by the wave of

Thorn's pistol. The snow glare of the aging afternoon faded behind them.

The cellar was dark and smelled of frozen mold. At first their eyes were useless. Moments later they adjusted in the absence of light and revealed the dimly lit corridors of their new surroundings. The walls were made of the same foundation stone as was the rest of the house. The ceiling was charred, and in some places it had collapsed, allowing shafts of sunlight to pierce the shadowy domain.

Huddled together for warmth and security, Meagan and the others—Thorn's gun still trained on them—watched as the old woman moved to the end of the twelve-foot corridor. A secreted door was exposed leading to steps which in turn would take them down further into the bowels of the ancient dwelling.

"I really don't like this," Julia murmured, as she and the others followed the old woman's lead with Thorn bringing up the rear.

"Just stay close. This isn't over yet," Delse confided softly to avoid being heard by Thorn.

The cavern below was much the same as the one above, only this one wound and snaked off in a dozen different directions. The walls here were wet from the floor up three feet to where the ground frost took over and held the moisture solid in frozen captivity.

*"About time you got here…"* The voice was little more than a whisper—so much so that it could have been imagined, yet it captured their attention as though announced through a bull horn.

"Did you guys hear that?" Meagan demanded, joining them in their search for the source. Thorn and the old lady had apparently been excluded from the greeting.

"Yeah, where'd it come from?" Delse asked.

Julia shook her head almost undetectably to say she also had no idea.

"Keep it moving up there," Thorn barked from the rear.

*"Don't worry. They can't hear me. Jus' you guys,"* the tiny voice, clearly that of a small child, whispered.

"Uhm, guys, I think I'm going crazy," Julia announced as calmly and as quietly as her newfound fear would allow.

"I think we all are," Meagan assured. "Just try to keep it down, will you?"

"Meagan's right. One problem at a time," Delse agreed.

While the others debated their sanity and the old lady led the way deeper and deeper into the bowels of the house, Meagan decided to try a crazy notion. Concentrating, she focused her thoughts: *"If you can hear me, speak only to me. The others are frightened."*

She thought as hard as she could without breaking a blood vessel.

*"Of course I can hear you,"* replied the tiny voice, and this time only Meagan could hear.

*"What is your name? Are you the same little girl we've all been dreaming about?"* Meagan thought.

*"My name is Mickey. Meagan, don't you remember me?"* the little voice sounded sad.

*"From the dreams. Of course,"* Meagan responded in her head.

*"No, before that. Remember, all four of us were here once. We had so much fun before that bad man spoiled it."*

Flashes of memory pulsated through Meagan brain. Memories of four small girls all thrown together in this dreadful place and forced to make the best of it. Memories of the fire and the events leading up to it filled her with long-forgotten hidden emotions, and once again, in an incredible flood of outrage and sadness, tears rolled her face.

"Meagan, what wrong?" Delse demanded, noticing the tears.

"I remember!" she sobbed freely, not caring who heard. "I remember what happened here!"

"What? How?" Julia seemed astounded.

"Mickey," was all Meagan said.

"Keep it down up there!" Thorn yelled.

Thorn's words no longer mattered to any of them. With the mention of Mickey's name, Julia and Delse's eyes widened with realization. Walls built up over a lifetime came crashing down, allowing the memories locked so tightly behind them to flow freely once more. Soon Meagan's tears were shared by Delse, and shortly thereafter by Julia. Why now? Surely each of them had mentioned that name at least once since they came to together, but now, in this place perhaps the will of the captive memories was now stronger than the lock barring their release.

"Okay, get in there!" Thorn commanded harshly.

Without any of them realizing, the old lady had stopped and now they stood next to a doorway carved into the rock.

"I think this has gone far enough!" Delse protested, staving back her tears.

"No one cares what you think!" Thorn snapped. "Get in there," he demanded, throwing Delse to the floor of the tiny cell. Meagan and Julia followed her in and the door was slammed and locked behind them.

"This really was a wondrous find, don't you think?" the old woman chirped, referring to the cell. "We'll be back in a short while and then we'll find out which of you my sister had the misfortune of giving birth to!" Her tone got considerably colder as she spoke.

"Your sister?" Julia spoke up, remembering how her own mother had died during childbirth.

"If you're looking for your sister's child and not your own, why all the fuss?" Delse asked.

"Because, you uneducated tramp. One of you killed her and when I find out which one I'll...well, you to figure out what will happen while we're gone."

"Wonderful," Meagan sighed. "Lady, you really are nuts. Anybody ever tell you that?"

"Hey! You shut up in there!" Thorn scolded.

"You go fuck yourself, Thorn!" Delse spat in Meagan's defense.

"I hope you're the one, Delse Collier. I am really going to enjoy cutting your guts out."

"Ah, come gimme me a kiss," she sneered, undaunted by his threat.

"Come along now, Mr. Thorn. We have much work to do before we meet with the doctors," the old woman prompted and moments later they were gone leaving Julia, Meagan and Delse alone.

In the corner of the small cell was an old and broken cot. Tattered cloth still clung to the

rusty mattress springs. There was nothing else. No windows, just a broken cot, a steel door and a damp sand floor.

"Mickey, are you still here?" Meagan asked, this time aloud, drawing curious glances from the others.

*"Yes, I'm here,"* came the reply, this time for all to hear. Again, her voice sounded sad.

"What's wrong? Why are you so sad?" Delse was surprised to hear herself ask.

*"Help me. Please, help me."*

"Mickey, how could we possibly help you? We can't even see you," Julia said, a little more than bewildered. All at once she wished she could take the words back. She had no desire to actually see the ghost of this little girl. However, no sooner were the words spoken when the answer became all too clear. "This is where it happened—isn't it?" Julia continued. There was no reply, but she knew she was on the right track. "This is where you died and with all the commotion during the fire they never found your body!" Julia was excited. She was on a roll. "You need our help to find it so you can rest." That last part she pulled right out of an old horror movie she once saw, but it seemed to fit, and since there was no supernatural rebuttal, she assumed she had guessed correctly. "Delse, can you get us out of here?"

Delse was looking at her as though she was looking at someone completely apart from their senses. "Should be able to," she said, pulling her kit out of her back pocket. "I'll give it a shot."

The lock in the door was new and offered little resistance against Delse's considerable experience in such matters. Moments later they were free.

"Okay, so now what?" Meagan asked, fearing the answer.

Suddenly, the vague image of a small child appeared in the entrance of another passage and the decision was made. The three exchanged an astonished glance and swallowed hard. Everything leading to this point had conditioned them— though perhaps not completely—to accept the appearance of this apparition. They followed.

The lighting in this stretch of tunnels was extremely poor. The only light came from a single lantern bolted to the wall in the passage they had just left. It cast their shadows ahead of them, hindering their sight. Finally, Julia reached into her pocket and removed her newly purchased cigarette lighter. Instantly, the shadows, opposed by the tiny flame, dispersed, exposing thick cobwebs hanging down from the ceiling and branching across the opening.

"I really hope that whatever made these is long since gone," Meagan said, quivering as she swept them away.

"Must have been one big mother of a spider," Delse affirmed.

"Thanks, Delse, I really needed to hear that!" Meagan quipped, moving beyond the glow of Julia's lighter.

The little wheel of the lighter grew increasingly warmer under Julia's thumb. She intended to allow her thumb to slide back onto the small orange plastic tab, but her hands were shaking and she misjudged— the flickering yellow flame disappeared. "Shit!" she exclaimed.

She struck the flint once again and it emitted a slight burst of spark. The flame sprang forth once more.

The tunnel ended and so did their search, for there lying against the stone wall were the skeletal remains of a small child.

Mickey's remains, still clad in a delicate, white cotton nightie. Together the women stood, both happy and saddened by their find. Sad, in the remembrance of Mickey's passing, and happy because now she too could find rest and the nightmare that had dominated each of their lives would end.

"Meagan? Meagan, are you down here?" a man's voice called out, sounding slightly winded.

"Down here, Bruce," she said.

"Oh, thank God!" he exclaimed as he rounded the bend into the tunnel and saw that each of them was all right. "The police caught Thorn and the old lady. Can you believe it? Their car got stuck in the drive…" Then his eyes fell upon the remains and his mouth went agape. "What … who is that?" he demanded, once the gift of speech was returned to him.

"This is… was… Mickey Jenson. She's the girl we've all been dreaming about these last weeks."

"Don't tell me shit like that! I won't sleep for a month!" he warned. "I'd better go tell the captain to get the coroner out here."

"Well, girls, tomorrow's Christmas Eve," Meagan began. "What do you say we take our lives back?"

"Sounds like a plan to me," Delse agreed.

"No argument here, either." This was from Julia.

"Well, now, isn't that a nice surprise," Delse teased.

They waited there in the tunnel a while longer. When an officer finally appeared, they turned their backs on the Forgiving Hearts Orphanage and all the hurt it had caused.

# CHAPTER 13

-Christmas Eve-

Delse stood next to Mike awaiting a response to their knock. He was still very weak, having only been released from the hospital that same afternoon.

As she stood there supporting him, she felt uncertain if she was indeed ready for what was to come next. Again, the urge to run was strong, but the time for running had gone, taking with it all those things that had once made life such a day-to-day ordeal.

The door opened and from within joyous warmth and smiling faces rushed up to meet the newest member of the family. Almost the instant their coats were removed, Mike and Delse were pulled apart and led in different directions—Mike to a comfortable chair where he could rest and Delse to a long sofa facing a roaring fireplace.

People seemed to come from everywhere, offering smiles, introductions and advice coupled with astonishment over Delse and Mike's exploits over the past weeks. It was all very overwhelming, to say the least. The questions flew at them like a freakish mortar barrage and would have continued had Mrs. Metcalf not stepped in.

"If you buzzards don't allow these kids a moment's peace this instant, I'm taking your presents back to the store." There was an edge to her voice, but no malice or actual intent to follow it through.

Delse smiled at the complete silence immediately following the threat. "Those must be great gifts," she mused.

"Come on, Delse. Come help me in the kitchen," Mrs. Metcalf said, taking her by the hand.

Delse hesitated, glancing over at Mike.

"Oh, don't worry about him. These yucks aren't as scary as they try to be," she added, and guided Delse from the room. "And someone get Mike a drink," she called back.

"You must have all sorts of questions yourself," Mrs. Metcalf said, handing Delse an apron.

"They can wait. All but one, that is …"

"Oh, and what might that one be?"

"Well … what do I call you?" Delse stumbled. "I mean, do I call you Mrs. Metcalf, or by your first name? What?"

"Well, you could call me Mom if you wanted to," Mrs. Metcalf replied, just as nervous as Delse of being rejected.

Tears appeared on Delse's face. She had needed to hear those words more than any others. Her heart soared. "I think Mom would be just fine," she replied, fighting to remain in control of her tears.

From that point on, Delse knew and would constantly be reminded that she did have a home and a mother who loved her deeply. Christmas could now be a joyous occasion for her again instead of one holding only regret and pain.

From the other room, a familiar sound crept into the kitchen. Someone was playing a piano accompanied by a chorus of voices raised in song.

It was Mike.

The voices were glorious, though horribly off-key, and as they rose through the house Delse knew beyond doubt that she had come home.

"Come on, let's go join in," Delse's mother prompted, leading the way back to the other room.

…AND ON EVERY STREET CORNER YOU HEAR … SILVER BELLS … SILVER BELLS … IT'S CHRISTMAS TIME IN THE CITY … RING-A- LING, HEAR THEM SING … SOON IT WILL BE CHRISTMAS DAY…"

Delse had come home.

# CHAPTER 14

-Christmas Day-

Meagan stood at the window of the Bathurst's front room gazing serenely into the distance.

She had forgotten just how much she truly loved it here. The smell of the house on holidays and special occasions, the crispness of the air outside able to hide even the most unpleasant offerings of the world at large. In the distance, Blue Mountain reached up and touched the sky with its delicate indigo lace. Even the clouds themselves were in awe of the wondrous hulks. They mirrored the ancient mammoths, presenting yet another more splendid range beyond the original.

She was home.

All that was around her confirmed it. And as she stood staring out into the distance she found it difficult, if not altogether impossible, to come up with a single valid reason to justify her former quest. Apart from the friendships fostered and the adventures shared, most everything else that had transpired during those last few weeks was now so very distant and unimportant.

Delse had found a new family and Julia went back to the life she had. Even Meagan, so bent on discovery, momentarily losing sight of what she had, was happy. What mattered most was here, in this very house.

Strange, she thought… it had taken such great lengths for her to realize something she had held as common knowledge most of her life.

"Meagan, dear, come along now. It's time to open the presents," Tina called from the doorway of the den.

Holding her gaze a moment longer, resolute that she would return to its beauty, and next time transfer it to canvas, Meagan answered Tina's summons and joined them in the den.

It was a cheerful room—one of her favorites. The dark-wood furniture, always polished to a deep shine, and the hand-knit throw cushions warmed by the glowing hearth always soothed her. As every other year before this, the tree stood prominently between two arching bay windows. It was adorned with a regalia of white lights, tiny red bows and a sea of glittering tinsel strands.

Below the tree, a barrage of brightly wrapped gifts waiting to be opened sparkled merrily under the gentle caress of three hundred tiny lights.

Tina stood next to the hearth and to her left sat Bruce and Craig. There was a strange feeling in the air, she thought, standing in the doorway sizing up the reception.

"Come on, dear, hurry up. Don't keep us all waiting," Tina urged, reaching for a manila collapsible file tightly bound with yellow cord that was on the mantle. "Craig and I have discussed this a great deal, and first of all we would like to apologize for not being there for you these last weeks. We are both truly sorry if we've caused you any pain and we'd like to try to make it up to you if we can."

"What she's trying to say is this," Craig jumped in. "If you still want to contact your biological parents we won't stand in your way any longer."

"Everything you should need is in this folder," Tina stated, handing it to her.

"Where was I born?" Meagan asked, staring blankly at the package.

"A little place called Hungry Hollow. Ironically, it's located not far from Sarnia." Tina replied.

"Are they dead or alive?"

"They're alive and well, though they're both married to different people."

"Sweetheart, I don't understand. All of these things are in the folder."

"Mom ... Dad ..." The words fell from her lips like joyous bells. "Thank you for this. Six months ago, it was the only thing you could have given me that I would have appreciated. Since then, however, I've come to learn a few things," she intoned. "Ever since I found out I was adopted and not your 'real' child I was haunted by it, because I thought I didn't know who I really was. The two of you always did, and I suspect Bruce did too, but I wasn't ready to listen then. These last weeks in Sarnia with Julia and Delse taught me something. They taught me that so long as I cling to the past there is no possible way I can ever have a future."

Tears glistened on Tina's face, and Craig's too, for that matter.

"Mom, Dad … if it's all right with you … can I go back to being your little girl again?"

Craig was the first to his feet. "You never stopped," he sighed lovingly, taking her in his arms.

"When do we get to open the prezzzants?" Bruce whined comically in an effort to lighten the mood.

"I'm with him!" Tina announced. "Let's get into 'em!"

Moments later the room was filled with the shrieks of joyous laughter and surprise as paper of every colour was torn mercilessly and cast to the floor.

"Meagan, here, put this by your chair so it doesn't get thrown out with the wrappings," Tina instructed, handing her the folder.

Meagan smiled. "Thanks, Mom." And with that, she leaned over and placed it squarely in the hearth. "I won't be needing it anymore."

Soon the flames were greedily consuming the time-dried parchments. With each page, each yellowed, black and white photograph that evaporated into shriveled black ash and drifted upward into the chimney a little more of the past released its hold on Meagan Bathurst.

# CHAPTER 15

Julia sat in her parent's winterized back porch leaning forward, a glass of scotch held loosely in her left hand, a largely ignored cigarette in her right. Dark circles had appeared under eyes red and swollen from too many tears.

Tommy's death, and the hand she had in it, combined now with the surfaced memories of Mickey and the old woman – her biological aunt – wanting her dead, and the pain she most certainly had caused the two people she loved most had set her mind in a loop of self-doubt … loathing. How could she ever go back to the life she had known in Sarnia? How could she be sure she wouldn't be the cause of another child's death? She wanted all of it to just go away.

"Figured I'd find you out here," her mother said. Glass of red wine in hand, she took a seat next to Julia and sat quietly for a moment.

"Where'd Dad go? I heard the car leaving the driveway."

"I sent him out for cranberry sauce."

"There are four cans of that stuff in the pantry."

"He doesn't know that," she said. Taking the cigarette from Julia's hand, she took a long deep drag and handed it back.

"I didn't know you smoke…" Julia said.

"Don't tell your father. Want to know something else?"

"What?

"Your dad and me … we're alright."

"Really, Mom?" she said. "I saw the hurt in your eyes when I told you about the first kidnapping…"

"What you saw wasn't hurt, it was concern for your safety," she said, taking the cigarette again. "That and an overwhelming desire to kill that bitch." She exhaled through her nose.

Julia sat in awe, watching this paradigm of all things virtuous, the one who, while growing up, she had always thought looked like the Statue of Liberty in the Paramount logo at the movies, smoke and swear and admit to murderous thoughts.

Becoming aware of Julia's gaze, her mom said, "What?"

"I am so going to need therapy!" Julia giggled.

"You got any more of these?" her mother asked before crushing the finished cigarette into a long- dead potted plant.

"Fill your boots," she said, handing over the pack.

There was a silence between them as the Statue of Liberty extracted a cigarette from the pack and lit it.

"Mom, I'm scared."

"I know you are, sweetheart."

"I'm not sure I can do it anymore … or that I even want to."

"Tommy?"

Julia nodded her head, looking deeply in the scotch she really hadn't wanted.

"So, then, what?" her mother asked. "You just going to sit out staring into a glass of cheap scotch you're never going to drink, holding cigarettes you don't intend to smoke?"

Julia allowed her head to fall forward. "Gawd! I'm a pathetic failure."

"Okay. Enough of this. As much as I've enjoyed your rather shaky impersonation of Hemingway, I need your help in the kitchen."

"Just like how you needed cranberry sauce?"

"Yes, exactly like how I needed cranberry sauce. Now, come on."

Setting the glass down, Julia followed her mother into the kitchen. "Hey, maybe I should do some travelling."

"Get away for awhile … get a new perspective," her mother agreed.

"Thanks, Mom."

"What for?"

"For the cranberry sauce."

# CHAPTER 16

## -April 8th –

The scent of thawing soil hung sweetly in the warm spring air. And while patches of the previous winter's snow still clung to the ground in ever-decreasing drifts, the trees had already started to adorn their branches with the promise of lush greens to come.

The minister's voice seemed to drift in from a great distance beginning deep in the heart of the endless sentinels of stone. His words held no importance—not really. It was the day—the warmth of the sun, the gentle caress of the breeze born of an early spring day, the peace and tranquility of this place nestled among rolling hills—that bore the importance.

"We commit the body of young Mickey Jenson ..." For a brief instant, his voice faded in and then just as quickly out again as thoughts of what lay behind Julia, Meagan and Delse washed over it.

Perched over the open grave was the small white casket in which lay Mickey's remains. Around it, dressed in the colours of mourning, five young souls stood watch over the ceremony of final farewell. The stone had already been placed and on it was a carving of a small white angel holding a single white rose.

Its inscription read:

THE INNOCENT SHALL POINT THE WAY
IN LOVING MEMORY
OF MICKEY JENSON

BORN 1966, DIED 1971
NEVER AGAIN TO BE FORGOTTEN

The service ended and the minister stepped back from the group. Together Meagan, Julia and Delse stepped forward and stood silently for a moment longer, their eyes red from tears. Each held a single red rose. One by one they stepped closer and placed their gift upon the casket. When the last rose had been placed, they turned to Mike and Bruce.

"It's done." Meagan smiled. "We can go now."

Silence ensued once more as they made their way back toward the car. In the fullness of time, their sadness would leave them and in its place fond memories of a young girl named Mickey Jenson would come. The events of their mutual past had haunted each of them. Now, however, its rein of fear, of dread, and of the profound sense not belonging, had ended. All of that was the past and if for no other purpose but to keep them ever-mindful of their mortal status, they had no need of it any longer. Ahead was only the future.

[THE END]

CPSIA information can be obtained
at www.ICGtesting.com
Printed in the USA
LVHW021658280920
667305LV00003B/687

9 781525 516436